Surviving The Pack

Written By
Rafael Garcia

Surviving The Pack

Copyright © 2024 by Rafael Garcia

For permissions requests, write to the author at the email address below:

Rafael Garcia email:

apositivedoseofralph@yahoo.com

Cover design: Rafael Garcia.

Interior design: Rafael Garcia.

Editor: Rafael Garcia.

Proofreader: Rafael Garcia.

Illustrations: Rafael Garcia.

ISBN: 979-8-218-34951-6

Printed in The United States.

First Edition: 2024

Printed on Premium Color Interior with white paper

About the Author

Rafael Garcia, a native of the humble city of San Antonio, Texas, he is not just an author but a beacon of resilience and inspiration. His journey, though marked by the arduous trials of living with Spinal Muscular Atrophy, a terminal medical condition, has not been defined by his disability but by his indomitable spirit and relentless optimism for life.

From an early age, Rafael learned to see beyond the constraints of his physical circumstances, discovering a world of infinite possibilities within the realm of imagination and the written word. It is his profoundly personal experiences with disability and depression that have shaped his poignant narratives, each one a testament to the power of hope, resilience, and the human spirit.

Rafael's work speaks directly to those grappling with despair, offering them a lifeline of understanding and empathy. He paints vivid pictures with his words, transforming his own tribulations into tales that inspire and uplift. His stories offer a unique perspective, encouraging readers not just to survive, but to thrive, reminding them always to seek the positives in life, no matter the challenge.

A man of deep faith, Rafael firmly believes in the sanctity of family. It is within the nurturing confines of his familial bonds that he has found the strength and motivation to overcome the battles life has thrown his way. His undying belief is that everyone owes it to themselves to strive for the best in this world, a philosophy that echoes through every page he writes.

Rafael's journey is a testament to the extraordinary feats that can be achieved when one refuses to be defined by their circumstances. His works stand as a symbol of hope for those battling depression, a true testament to the power of resilience, and a reminder of the inherent beauty in life's most difficult moments.

Rafael Garcia is more than an author. He's a voice of hope, an advocate for being yourself no matter what, a narrative of strength, and an embodiment of faith. As you turn the pages of his works, prepare to be inspired, to find strength in adversity, and to be reminded of the unyielding power of the human spirit that lay within us all.

Dedication to my Mother Yvonne Garcia,

This book is firstly dedicated to you, Mom, with profound gratitude and immeasurable love. Throughout my life, you have been a guiding influence, teaching me invaluable lessons about faith, true faith, and spirituality. Your unwavering belief in something greater than ourselves has shaped my worldview, giving me strength during challenging times and reminding me of the power of hope.

For over 28 years, you have been my mentor, imparting wisdom and knowledge that transcends mere words. Your teachings on sacrifice, and I mean true sacrifice, have shown me the importance of selflessness and putting others before oneself. Through your actions, you have exemplified the true meaning of dedication, teaching me to commit fully to my goals and never give up, no matter the obstacles.

Your love, Mom, has been a force that has molded me into the man I aspire to be. The unconditional love you have showered upon me has been the bedrock of my confidence and self-worth. It is this very love that I hope to one day pass on to my own future family, just as you have done for me.

I want to express my deepest gratitude for simply being the incredible mother that you are. Your nurturing nature, your unwavering support, and your unwavering belief in my potential have been the front pillar of my life. You have been an inspiration to me every step of the way, showing me the boundless possibilities that await when one embraces life with an open heart.

Mom, this book is a testament to the impact you have made on my life. You have shaped me in ways that words cannot fully capture. As I embark on this journey of sharing my creativity and passion with the world, I carry your teachings and love within me. This is my humble way of saying thank you for everything you have done, and continue to do, for me.

With all my love and utmost appreciation,

Your son, Rafael Garcia (Mijo)

In dedication to my dear sister Arlene Womble,

I want to take a moment to express my deepest gratitude for all that you have done for me throughout my life. You have been a constant source of love, support, and encouragement, and I cannot thank you enough for all that you have done.

I will never forget when I was just a 12-year-old boy and I was afraid to express myself. You told me to live life the way I should and to never let fear hold me back. That advice has stayed with me throughout my life, and I am so grateful for your wisdom and guidance.

You have always been the person who reminded me of how great of a writer I was and believed in me no matter what. Your everlasting support has helped shape me into the man I am today, and I am forever grateful for your presence in my life.

And let's not forget your amazing cooking skills! Your egg rolls are truly the best in the world, and I always look forward to enjoying them whenever we are together.

Thank you, Arlene, for being an amazing sister and for all that you have done for me. I love you more than words can ever express.

With love and appreciation,

Rafael Garcia. (Nae)

In dedication to my brothers Alvaro Ramirez and Ricardo Garcia,

To Ricardo and Alvaro, my brothers, my guides, my warriors. You taught me the most valuable lessons of life, not by lecturing but by living. You showed me how to stand tall as I had to face some pretty tough odds, not by words but by actions. You both lit my path with your unstoppable courage, resilience, and the sheer will to never give up. You both taught me that my disability is not a barrier, but a unique part of me, something that only amplifies my positive attitude and determination.

Your love and companionship have been my lanterns in the darkest of nights. You have been there for me during my battles, not as spectators, but as soldiers, fighting alongside me. You have been my solace in my struggles, my joy in my sorrows. You brought me pizza when I was sick many times, a simple act of kindness that spoke volumes about your love for me. You took me to the movies when I was down, and depressed, a gesture that lifted my spirits and reminded me of the brighter side of life.

Your selfless actions, your boundless love, and your relentless optimism have been the back beacons of hope to my life. You taught me to smile, not despite the struggles but because of them. You taught me to celebrate my uniqueness, to embrace my individuality, and to cherish my abilities.

Every moment with you, every memory we've built, every lesson you've taught me, I will carry with me until my very last breath. Your love, your support, your guidance, have made me who I am today.

To Rick and Al, this book is not just dedicated to you guys, but it is a testament of my love for you, a tribute to your immeasurable faith, and a celebration of the bond we share. Thank you for making my journey worthwhile. I am who I am, because you both have been you. Here's to you, my brothers.

PS: stop calling me Iron man, and talking about the Mavericks.

With much love, and appreciation your brother.

Rafael Garcia (Ralph)

My letter to God

I am profoundly grateful to the Almighty, to God, for His infinite blessings and guidance throughout my journey. His presence has been a constant source of strength and inspiration, leading me through every triumph and challenge I have encountered. With deepest humility, I express my heartfelt gratitude for His never-ending support in the creation of this book and in shaping my life.

I sit here in awe of the countless ways in which God has touched my existence. His grace has illuminated my path, enabling me to navigate the darkest of times and emerge stronger. His love has embraced me, providing solace and comfort during moments of despair. His wisdom has guided my decisions, instilling within me a sense of purpose and clarity.

This book is a testament to God's boundless mercy and faithfulness. It is through His divine intervention that I have been granted the ability to share my creativity, knowledge, and insights with others. Every word penned on these pages is a testament to His grace, for without His guiding hand, this endeavor would have not even been possible.

As I reflect upon my life's journey, I am reminded that this book is but a small chapter in the grand narrative that God has scripted for me. It is a privilege to have been given the opportunity to pour my heart and soul into these words, and I am eternally grateful for His assistance throughout the creative process.

I acknowledge that no matter where I go from here, in this book or in life, it is all mere icing on the cake. God has already blessed me abundantly, and everything that follows is an additional gift from His benevolent hands. I humbly accept these blessings, knowing that they are a reflection of His boundless love and generosity.

In conclusion, I offer my deepest gratitude to God for His immeasurable blessings, guidance, and unending love. May His divine presence continue to illuminate my path as I embark upon new journeys, knowing that with His grace, all things are possible.

With heartfelt appreciation and reverence,

Rafael Garcia

Warning:

Content Advisory for Individuals Struggling with Depression and PTSD.

This book contains highly intense and sensitive content that may not be suitable for individuals currently experiencing depression or post-traumatic stress disorder (PTSD). We strongly advise exercising caution if you are in a vulnerable mental state or actively seeking professional help for these conditions. Here are important points to consider before proceeding:

1. Graphic Depictions of Traumatic Events: This book vividly portrays traumatic events and the harsh realities of survival in mentally challenging circumstances. It includes scenes that may be distressing, unsettling, or triggering to those who have experienced trauma. The content explores themes of blood, gore, and foul language within the context of individuals trying to survive in extreme situations.

2. Emotional Impact and Triggering Content: The explicit nature of the content may evoke strong emotions, including fear, anxiety, and sadness. The book delves into the depths of mental anguish and the struggles of the characters, which may resonate with your personal experiences. Please be aware that engaging with such material can potentially intensify your emotional state or trigger memories associated with your own trauma.

3. Lack of Clinical Guidance: It is crucial to emphasize that this book is a work of fiction and does not replace professional advice, therapy, or support. The author's portrayal of mental health challenges and trauma survival should not be considered as clinical guidance. We strongly recommend consulting with mental health professionals or support networks to ensure you receive appropriate care tailored to your specific needs.

4. Self-Care and Support: Engaging with this book may require implementing self-care strategies and establishing a strong support system. Take breaks, when necessary, practice self-care techniques, and reach out to trusted individuals who can provide emotional support during and after reading.

5. Trauma Triggers and Sensitivity: This book may contain explicit descriptions of traumatic events, violence, and harsh language. Proceed with caution, considering your own personal triggers and sensitivity to such content. If you find yourself becoming overwhelmed or experiencing distressing symptoms, it is vital to prioritize your well-being and seek immediate assistance from a mental health professional or helpline.

Remember, your mental health and well-being take precedence over any book or narrative. If you are currently struggling with depression or PTSD, we encourage you to prioritize your recovery and consult with a mental health professional before engaging with potentially triggering content.

If you need immediate assistance or are in crisis, please contact your local mental health helpline or emergency services. You are not alone, and support is available to help you through difficult times.

You are not alone.

Preface

Surviving The Pack has been a ten-year journey for me, and I am thrilled to finally share it with the world. When I first began writing this book I had no idea how closely the story of Arthur Peters, a survivalist living in the Alaskan wilderness, would parallel my own journey through life. As a person living with Spinal Muscular Atrophy (SMA), I have faced numerous challenges that have tested my resilience and determination. Yet it wasn't until I began writing this story that I truly understood the power of faith in overcoming adversity.

In "Surviving the Pack," our protagonist, Arthur Peters, is a skilled survivalist and adventurer who has chosen later in life to live a life of solitude in the vast, unforgiving landscape of Alaska. Living off the land, he relies on his wits and experience to navigate the challenges he faces. But when Arthur finds himself facing the specter of death itself, he must dig deep within to find the strength to carry on.

In many ways like I said, Arthur's journey mirrors my very own. Diagnosed with my disability at a young age, I have been forced to confront my own mortality on a daily basis, grappling with the limitations of my physical body while striving to maintain my independence and dignity. Just as Arthur must use his survival skills to tackle the challenges that the Alaskan forest sends his way, I too have had to rely on my inner resources to overcome the obstacles that SMA has placed in my path.

It is my hope that "Surviving the Pack" serves as a testament to the power of perseverance and the indomitable human spirit. For both Arthur and myself, the key to survival lies not in just our physical prowess but in our inner faith to never give up hope, even in the face of seemingly impossible odds. Through Arthur's story, I aim to inspire readers to embrace their own challenges with courage and tenacity, knowing that the true measure of a person is not in the trials they face but in how they choose to overcome them.

As both the author and a survivor, I invite you to join Arthur Peters on his harrowing journey through the Alaskan wilderness, and to discover the resilience and strength that lie within each and every one of us. May the story of "Surviving the Pack" serve as a reminder that, no matter the challenges we face, we must never give up hope.

Rafael Garcia

Table of Contents

Chapter One: 1

Chapter Two: 12

Chapter Three:.. 19

Chapter Four: 24

Chapter Five: 36

Chapter Six:... 48

Chapter Seven:... 71

Chapter Eight: 94

Chapter Nine: 108

Chapter Ten:.. 121

Chapter One:

The Hunter Becomes
the Hunted

Arthur Peters had always been a solitary man. He preferred the quiet of the wilderness to the hustle and bustle of the city, and he had spent most of his late adult life living off the land. He was a survivalist, and he had honed his skills over the years to become one of the best.

Arthur had been living alone in a cabin in the mountains of Alaska for several months now. Where he had chosen the location because it was remote and far from civilization. He had stocked up on enough supplies to last him for a year, and he had moved into this sturdy shelter so that he could withstand even the harshest of weather.

But one night, everything changed. Arthur was sitting by the fire, sipping on a cup of tea, when he heard a strange noise outside. He immediately grabbed his rifle and stepped out of his front door to investigate.

As he peered into the darkness of the vast cold night, he saw a pack of wolves circling his cabin. He knew he was in trouble. Wolves were notorious predators in these parts, and they were not afraid to attack humans.

Arthur steadied his heart rate as he could feel it begin to rise. His blood began to run cold like the temperature that was outside of his cabin.

Even though Arthur was an experienced hunter, he had only become familiar with small game throughout his years of learning, and never had come across a pack of animals like these beasts that currently stood in front of him.

He knew that he was no match for the large numbers of this pack of wolves. In response he tried to scare them off by firing his rifle into the air, but they only growled and snarled as they answered his warning.

He retreated back slowly into his cabin and locked the door, hoping that the wolves would eventually lose interest and leave him alone. But they were persistent, and they continued to howl and scratch at the door throughout the night.

Arthur laid on his bed with the feelings of dread flooding through his body like nothing he'd ever felt before. Sure, he had encountered things in the past with his experiences, but this felt like truly something unfamiliar to him.

He barely slept that night, and when he awoke in the morning, he noticed the wolves were gone, but the feeling of unease still lingered. Arthur knew he needed to take action so he spent the next day fortifying his cabin. He reinforced the door and windows with extra planks of wood, and he set up traps around the perimeter of his property.

Later that same evening, Arthur was enjoying a nice meal with his best friend solitude, along with a bottle of whiskey to tickle his taste buds. He enjoyed a hearty meal of ribeye steak with a baked potato to accompany the smooth rich Alcohol. As he sat enjoying a wholesome meal, he flipped through an old hunting magazine he had been saving to read.

But as the survivalist sat there with the big dinner, it quickly found itself forgotten like Arthur had been forgotten from the world. The fading steam of the steak was now a mere afterthought as his mind swirled with a torrent of struggles.

The hunting magazine was finding the same fate, its pages that were filled with tales of triumph and survival, just lay open in front of him, but his gaze had drifted aimlessly, unable to focus on the words. The only sound that punctuated the uneasy silence was the distant songs of the wind, an eerie chorus that seemed to mirror the turmoil growing within Arthur's heart.

His intense gaze shifted restlessly toward the cabin's windows; his mind consumed by a relentless sense of urgency. Outside, hidden among the trees, he knew lurked the wolves, the relentless predators who had now marked him as their prey. The memory of their piercing yellow eyes, glinting with feral hunger, now haunted his every waking moment.

Arthur's fingers clenched tightly into a fist, while his loyal companion that was named solitude whispered the thoughts of his own mortality running over him. His entire being yearned for the traps he had set around the perimeter, hoping against hope that they would serve as a formidable defense, a barrier between him and the relentless jaws of the beasts that now stalked his home.

Each creak and groan of the cabin's aging structure sent shivers down his spine, his senses now on high alert, attuned to the smallest disturbance. The walls seemed to whisper their own secrets, tales of the Alaskan landscape that had already an endless planta of stories that had come before him, their battles for survival etched into the very fiber of the woods around where he had placed himself.

With every passing moment, the tension within Arthur grew, his heart pounding within his chest like a wild drumbeat. The isolation of the cabin, once a source of solace, now felt like a prison, amplifying his vulnerability. He yearned for the reassurance of reinforcements, the comforting presence of the former life he had before his survival journey who had pledged to stand by his side.

In the flickering firelight, shadows danced and twisted, casting uncanny shapes upon the walls. Arthur's mind conjured images of the wolves, their sleek bodies gliding silently through the underbrush, their piercing howls echoing through the horrors of this ungodly night. He wondered if the traps would hold, if he would be granted a momentary respite from the relentless pursuit of the event's that were beginning to grow darker as the more time passed.

Despite the uncertainty that threatened to engulf him, Arthur clung to a flicker of hope. Hope that the traps would snare the wolves, hope that reinforcements would magically arrive before the night was swallowed by the jaws of danger. He craved for the dawn, when the first rays of sunlight would pierce through the darkness, banishing the nightmares that now plagued him.

But until then, as he sat alone in that cabin, his magazine forgotten and his dinner barely touched, Arthur knew that the wolves were just beyond his door, their primal hunger driving them ever closer. And so, he steeled himself for the long and treacherous night that lay ahead, praying that his traps and reinforcements would prove enough to protect him from the jaws of his relentless pursuers.

And as the hours began to work their way later into the darkness of the night, he decided to clean up, and then take a nice hot shower.

While Arthur stood there beneath the cascading water in his warm rustic cabin, the steam was enveloping him in a comforting embrace. The rhythmic sound of the shower provided a brief respite from the harsh realities of the wilderness that had surrounded him. But even in this fleeting moment of tranquility, his mind was unmoved, and couldn't escape the persistent thoughts of this relentless pack that was still lurking on the outskirts of not just his property, but on his already heavy exhausted mind.

As the water washed away the grime and sweat of his daily routine, Arthur's unease only grew. The echoes of the distant cries reverberated in his once sharp intellect, reminding him of the wood's primal nature that moved with stealth just beyond the safety of his fortress of solitude. He couldn't shake the feeling that the wolves were now closing in, their predatory eyes fixed upon his already vulnerable mental state.

With the cabin's reinforced door still looming in his thoughts, Arthur's mind continued to race with heavy doubt. Had he done enough to fortify this sanctuary? Were the extra planks even sturdy enough to keep out the determined pack of hungry predators? His palms became slippery with anxiety, causing him to clutch the shower handle tighter as he tried to steady his nerves.

Even though Arthur had spent years honing his survival skills, meticulously preparing for the unknown, and had stockpiled food, fortified his shelter, and learned the secrets of the wilderness. He was quickly finding out that even the most seasoned survivalist had moments of vulnerability, moments when the weight of the unknown pressed upon their shoulders.

The sound of falling water only intensified as Arthur's heartbeat quickened. He closed his eyes, visualizing the cabin's walls as impenetrable barriers, impervious to the outside world that had already damaged him. He reminded himself of the countless nights he had already spent huddled by his fireplace, listening to the crackling logs and feeling the warmth chase away the chill of the wilderness.

Determined to regain his composure, Arthur turned off the shower and stepped onto the worn wooden floorboards. Droplets of the water glistened on his skin as he reached for the towel, wrapping himself in its comforting embrace. He glanced out the frosted window, seeing only the dense forest that lay beyond.

The snow of the Alaskan weather was heavy, but not as heavy as his already worn-out spirit.

While he sighed with weariness, Arthur had now turned his attention to the bathroom sink where he began shaving the stubble to his growing beard, when without notice he began to hear the unmistakable growling of the wolves that had now returned to his front door. The growls mixed with the cold howl of the already chilled air was causing an otherworldly experience to say the least. Arthur quickly wiped the remains of shaving cream he had on his face and hurriedly grabbed his rifle where he cracked the door open just enough to feed his weapon through, and once again shot into the emptiness that laid beyond of this already darkened night of turmoil.

But the wolves were unstoppable. They continued to circle his cabin, waiting for an opportunity to take advantage of the man that lay inside awaiting them.

"Go away, just leave me alone now!" Arthur screamed through the walls of his home as if the cold blooded predators could understand his very words. He wasn't thinking rationally with himself nor his skillset. The heavy cry of the wind was like God reminding him to calm down.

But he couldn't, and Arthur now found he was losing the remains of his focus, and the mental war running rampant within him. The survivalist was no longer a survivalist at this point in time. He was only a man gripped with pure, and utter fear. Any choice from this moment going forward could only be an endless string of errors on his behalf.

Arthur knew that in his current frame of mind he couldn't stay holed up in his cabin forever. He needed to find a way to escape this growing madness and make his way out to call for safety. He knew that time was of the essence as the hunger of these predators awaited him.

Arthur spent the next few days continuing to study the wolves behavior. He observed their movements and tried to anticipate their next attempt. He knew that he needed to be patient and wait for the right moment to make sure he had a handle on the situation.

Finally, on the fifth day, everything took a turn for the worst. The wolves had grown bolder, pressing their weight at the door more and snarling as they had now ventured closer, all the while knowing it was tormenting his fragile mind. Arthur knew that if he didn't get ahold of his thoughts soon, he would have to act fast.

When he looked outside his window, the pack of wolves had now gathered around a tree just a few meters from his door, their glowing eyes and haunting howls continuing on filling the forest, and his mental capacity. They would still approach where they would claw endlessly at the surface entrance, their desperation more evident as they sought to break in. Arthur's heart still raced, his mind filled with so many conflicting emotions. Fear gnawed at him, his instinct for self-preservation urged him to stay inside the safety of his cabin.

But as the wolves had persisted, their determination unyielding, Arthur unexpectedly felt a different emotion bubbling up within him—compassion. He had always respected and admired the wild creatures that roamed the surrounding forests. In his time of solitude, he had observed other game from afar, recognizing their place in the delicate balance of nature.

Arthur approached the door, his hands trembling as he reached out to touch the wood. The wolves' growls and snarls once more had intensified, their primal instincts urging them to claim their prey and his shelter that lay just beyond their reach. With a deep breath, Arthur spoke, his voice filled with a mixture of fear and resolve.

"Leave! You must fucking leave! This is supposed to be my home, my sanctuary!"

The wolves responded with ferocious howls, their cries drowning out Arthur's words. Their determination was unrelenting, refusing to yield to his pleas. Arthur's heart sank, realizing that his words alone would not dissuade them any longer. He needed to take action.

Gathering his thoughts, Arthur weighed his options one more time. Leaving the cabin would mean abandoning the safety he had built for himself. It would mean confronting the dangers and uncertainties of the wild, facing the harsh elements and other potential predators. But staying inside meant denying the very essence of his being—a deep-rooted connection with nature and a respect for the creatures that inhabited it.

In the midst of the cacophony outside, Arthur made up his mind.

To say ignorance was bliss was a true understatement as the now emotionally unstable man made the biggest error he could ever possibly make.

He grabbed his rifle with its remaining ammunition in the guns magazine, and a backpack filling it with as much supplies he could carry in a hurry, and he made a run for it. The wolves were caught off guard as the survivalist burst out the front door, and running with a surge of adrenaline coursing through his body. He managed to make it a few hundred yards before they caught up to him.

He turned around and fired his rifle, hitting one of the wolves in the leg. It yelped in pain and fell to the ground, giving Arthur a momentary reprieve.

He continued to run, dodging trees and rocks as he made his way deeper into the unknown Alaskan forest. He could hear the wolves howling behind him, getting closer and closer with each passing moment.

Arthur knew that he couldn't keep up this pace forever. He needed to find a place to hide and regroup. He spotted a small cave a few yards ahead and made a beeline for it.

As he crawled Into the cave and huddled in a corner, catching his breath. He could hear the wolves lashing out and scraping at the entrance, but he knew that they couldn't get in. At least not yet.

And just like any desperate human in a situation of pure survival, Arthur found himself there alone in the deep hearted wilderness, with little supplies and only a few remaining rounds in his rifle.

"what the fuck was I thinking. How could I have been so fucking stupid." Arthur mumbled to himself as he realized he had nobody to blame for this act of brainless feed, but himself.

"I'm not going to die here. I can't, I need to somehow fight." Arthur said to himself as he looked on staring at the already leering pack, and their glowing eye's that stared on from the outside.

He leaned against the rough damp walls of the cave, while he could still hear the frustrated snarls and howls of the wolves at the surface entrance. Arthur felt slight relief that the narrow entrance made it impossible for them to get in for now, but that didn't stop them from circling the mouth of the cave, eager for a chance to tear into Arthur's flesh. Their menacing growls and the rustling of their fur as they paced back and forth sent shivers down his spine, a stark reminder of the life or death situation he now found himself in.

Despite the terror that had gripped him, exhaustion began to take its toll. Arthur's limbs felt heavy, and his vision blurred as he fought to keep his eyes open. He slid down the wall, resting his head against the cold stone, as the wind outside picked up.

The gusts howled through the trees, creating an eerie symphony with the sounds of the beasts.

Slowly, the chilling wind and the haunting cries of these monsters began to lull Arthur into a restless slumber. His mind drifted in and out of consciousness, as dreams and reality seemed to merge into one. The fierce snarls of the wolves morphed into the distant call of a siren, beckoning him into the depths of the unknown.

As the night wore on, Arthur's body finally succumbed to the exhaustion, and he fell into a deep sleep. In his dreams, he roamed the Alaskan forest as he was hunted by endless numbers of wolves. They'd attempt to catch him at every turn he'd make. The glow of their eyes piercing into his very soul. Arthur could feel his dance with death move through the wind's of the very fibers of his spirit.

Just as he thought he'd gotten away a pair of razor-sharp teeth would sink into his neck startling the survivalist awake.

Arthur found it a relief to know that the wolf that had clung it's piercing fangs into his flesh was only just a dream.

But that didn't mean the actual reality was still not without its own dangers. The cold continued to seep into the cave, numbing Arthur's skin and creeping into his bones. He shivered in his semi sleep state, his body's desperate attempt to stay warm in the face of death continued on, but little did he know that the end was far away. Because this story was just beginning.

Chapter Two:

The Attack

Arthur took a deep breath and checked his backpack for what was already the umpteenth time. He only had a few supplies left, including an empty water bottle, a fire striker, two protein bars, a first aid kit, and a flashlight. He had been trapped inside the cave for two days now, and the wolves outside were getting more aggressive as time continued to pass by. He had managed to shoot one of them with his rifle, as he ran his way to the cave, but once there he found himself trapped.

Every time Arthur thought the area was clear he'd try to make an attempt to escape, but the constantly driven, and savage animals would chase him back inside. This action would let him know that if he couldn't be their meal he was going to be their prisoner.

As time continued to grow, his life started a downwards trajectory between two choices, trying to fight or let himself die where he was placed. So, there he was, in a cold empty cave with nothing but isolation by his side. He knew that he was running out of time and ammunition fast. He needed to find a way out before the wolves got to him.

While the middle-aged man in his 40's crouched there with his internal struggles, he knew it was now or never. Arthur started to formulate a plan to take these beast down.

He knew he needed to go to a place he had been avoiding. But just before the rage began to reach it's boiling point he heard the familiar rustle of twigs clattering at the snowy ground outside the forest.

Arthur sat there, and listened closely to the wolves howling deep within the tree's and he knew that they were once again going to try to get to him. He could feel his heart racing as he realized that this was probably going to be his last chance to attempt any form of escape.

As he sat down there, his mind suddenly raced with thoughts of fear and panic. He knew that he had to come up with something fast, but his mind was clouded with the terror of the situation. He tried to think of ways to escape, but every idea he came up with seemed impossible. He was trapped, and the wolves were not going to back down.

Arthur could feel his palms growing sweaty and his breath becoming shallow. He knew that he had to remain calm and focused if he was going to make it out of this situation alive. He tried to slow his breathing and clear his mind, but the sound of the pack continuously howling outside was too overwhelming.

Despite his fear, Arthur knew that he couldn't just sit still in this cave and wait for the wolves to attack. He had to face his real life nightmare, and make a plan that would result in his very own survival. He took a deep breath and braced himself for what was to come.

The poor Survivor knew that this was probably going to be his end, but he'd be damn sure if he wasn't going to go down giving every bit of fight in his body he had left.

He picked up his rifle, checked the remaining rounds in the magazine, and took a deep breath. He knew that he had to be quick and precise if he wanted to take down the wolves.

Then in a flash, he heard a loud thud on the cave wall, and he knew that the wolves were going to finally break through. He aimed his weapon at the entrance and waited for the ferocious pack to strike. An unearthly calmness covered the air like a blanket from God himself. Arthur closed his eyes softly taking a moment that was soon followed by the wolves charging inside with a high velocity towards him, baring their sharp teeth and growling menacingly.

Arthur took what he assumed could be his last breath, and with all his courage started shooting. He managed to take down three wolves with his first three shots, but he knew that he had to be more careful now. He waited for the wolves to get closer and aimed for their heads. He managed to take down two more relentless hounds before he ran out of his ammunition.

The remaining rabid animals leaped high in the air attacking him, one scratched Arthur's face giving the man a deep laceration on his forehead. He fell onto his back with a hard impact. The other wolf seeing this took the opportunity and attacked his leg clenching into his calf with its razor-sharp teeth and scratching its deep claws into his leg. Arthur screamed in pain, and knew that he had to fight back with whatever he had left.

He picked up a rock and repeatedly struck the sharpened edge of the heavy set stone at the wolf biting at his leg on the skull. Blow after blow Arthur screamed as he gave the animal every wallop he had in him, eventually making it fall to the ground lifeless. Arthur then quickly picked up another one, but this time it was a much sharper stone with a cleaner edge to it and with his full weight he stabbed the other beast straight into the chest.

"Ah!" Arthur screamed as his now blood covered face showed that he was not just ready for a fight, but he was ready for a war if needed.

The other wolves backed off, sensing that Arthur was not going to he an easy prey for them. They turned quickly retreating back into the depths of the Alaskan woods.

Now that he was finally alone, Arthur took a deep breath trying to calm himself down and came to realize that he was badly hurt. He had deep cuts and teeth marks on his leg, and his hands were trembling badly. He was aware that he had to find a way to stop the bleeding and make a fire to keep his own survival going. He knew that it was important, and he needed to stabilize himself as much as he could.

Arthur with his still trembling hands reached for his first aid kit and was thankful to see that he had a staple gun, some ointment, and bandages. Trying to calm himself down, Arthur steadied his hands from shaking, then quickly took the staple gun, and rapidly began stapling his wounds as fast as he could, trying not to think about it nor the immense pain it brought. "Ah God!" Arthur screamed with each click of the medical grade device hoping for it to be over soon.

When it was finally over, Arthur saw his hands were now painted in his own blood, and the wounds on his leg were closed and temporarily mended. But while the survivor tried with all his might to calm down from the unbearable pain coursing through him, Arthur recognized that his life was still balancing on the line of death.

Knowing his still dire predicament was still growing, Arthur reached for the medication with his trembling hands looking to gain any sort of relief from his never-ending dance with the dangers he was facing.

Once he was done unscrewing the cap to the tube, Arthur slowly started applying the antiseptic ointment over the area he had stapled, and then began wrapping his leg with bandages.

Following his multiple ordeals of suffering, the wounded and recovering Arthur now found himself there in a long period of sitting in the cave waiting. He wanted to make sure that the wolves were gone for good. It was the best thing to do before he even decided to attempt to head out to further safety, but little did he know that this fight was still far from over.

With time he picked up his flashlight and started looking for a way out of the cave gingerly, but still very weak. Arthur could feel the weight of his bodies straining muscles from each movement as he tried to walk, causing extreme aches across his entire body.

After several minutes of searching for the entrance, he was relieved to find it, but he collapsed from exhaustion hitting the ground hard, and was unable to walk any further.

Arthur now found himself needing to now crawl towards the caves opening, as he now had lost his ability to walk or even stand due to the storm of pain that rained down on him.

Still even in the midst of his struggle he managed to squeeze through the opening and finally found himself outside, in the cold and dark night.

Following the initial attack, Arthur couldn't stop seeing red, but as he looked around as best as he could, he saw a small stream nearby. He crawled towards it desperate to get fluids into his now dehydrated body.

Once he made it to the stream, the damaged, and broken man realized the extent of his trauma as he looked into the reflection of the clear liquid of life. In return he saw the crimson mask that mixed with his hair and sweat, with frozen mucus that now covered every fiber of his face.

And with that Arthur couldn't hold it in any longer. The lone survivor let out what only could be described as a deep piercing, and primal scream of pain not just from his wounds, but the opening of his soul.

As the tears of his spirit rained down over the man, he gradually dipped his face into the fresh oasis that laid before him. Arthur could feel immediate relief when the feeling of the cold water hit his skin. He drank copious amounts of it and then collapsed to his side on the ground exhausted.

While he laid on his back with nothing, but pain and exhaustion singing together in a harmonious tune to let him know of the seriousness his body was experiencing, Arthur knew that his life was now hanging on by a mere thread.

Arthur was aware that he had survived the attack but he also knew that he had to survive the night, but most importantly he had a long way to go before he could reach civilization. He closed his eyes and took a deep breath, knowing that he had to just keep pushing forward, and do the one thing he knew he was born to do, and that's live.

Chapter Three:

The Race For Shelter

As the night wore on, Arthur's pain only grew worse. He tried to keep his mind occupied by thinking of all the survival skills he had learned over the years, but the agony was just too intense. He could feel his body growing weaker, and he knew that he needed to find a way to get help before it was too late. With a deep breath, Arthur slowly sat up as best as he could and surveyed his surroundings. His worn body was still by the stream, but the snow was falling heavier now, and he knew that he needed to build a shelter soon if he was going to make it through the night. He looked around for any signs of animal tracks or human habitation, but he saw nothing.

He was thankful there were no signs of the wolves for the time being, but he was still on high alert.

Arthur recognized that he needed to act fast if he wanted to survive in this unappeasable wilderness. He took a deep breath and assessed his situation. He was injured, exhausted, and alone. He had nothing but his empty rifle, a water bottle, a fire striker, two protein bars, and a half used first aid kit. He cursed himself for making the rookie mistake of not packing enough supplies before running away from the wolves. When everything had started the survivalist didn't think of his skill, but sadly he let the fear with panic override his mind instead of the years of training he had went through.

He took another deep breath and tried to calm himself down. Panic would only make matters worse as they've already had done. He knew he needed to focus on building a shelter and getting a fire going. That would be his only chance of surviving the harsh conditions of these unforgiving wood's.

Arthur struggled to get himself up, using his rifle as support. He knew he had to keep moving if he wanted to survive the unforgiving cold. He hobbled along the riverbank, but with each step his leg continued to throb, and furthermore the persistent bleeding on his face still lingered.

The man's shirt, and jacket was nothing, but now a blood stained mess. Still Arthur refused to give up. He closed his eye's softly, and took another deep breath before whispering with a authoritative tone to himself. "Fuck it, I'm not going to die here."

He bent down, and opened up the first aid kit, and with quick fashion like his leg he stapled his forehead with sixteen staples into his face.

Arthur tried his best not to scream as he was biting into his collar of the heavy coated winter jacket he wore. The poor man couldn't help himself, and cried with every unrelenting click as the staples made their way into his open wounds.

Once he was done he wrapped up his forehead tight. Arthur felt dizzy momentarily as he tried to Once again take a few steps, and was aware he most likely suffered a concussion from the attack, but he had to keep venturing forward without wasting anymore time.

He started by looking for a suitable spot to build his shelter. He soon felt a slight wave of relief as he found a small clearing with a few trees nearby. He knew that he needed to find a spot that was sheltered from the wind and had enough dry wood and leaves to use as insulation.

He gathered some dry branches and leaves and started building a lean-to shelter against the trunk of two large trees. He used the rest of his first aid kit to fashion a makeshift rope from the bandages and tied the branches together to form a sturdy frame. He then covered the frame with the remaining leaves and branches, leaving a small opening for him to crawl inside.

Once the shelter was complete, he started gathering wood for his fire. He knew that he needed to get the fire going to keep warm and to signal for help if anyone was nearby. He found some dry twigs and small branches and used his empty water bottle to collect some more water from the stream that still was in close proximity.

Arthur then used his persistence skillset to start a fire using the fire striker and some of the dry grass he had collected. The fire crackled and roared to life, sending warmth and light into his shelter. Arthur felt a sense of relief wash over him as he sat down next to the gentle flame as he sipped his water finally getting a moment to rest.

He knew he needed to rest and recover from his injuries, but he also knew that he needed to remain on the lookout for any more signs of danger. He used the scope of his rifle to scan the surrounding area, keeping a watchful eye for any movement.

While he sat there, surrounded by the quiet of the wilderness, Arthur felt a sense of peace wash over him under the Alaskan sky. He knew that he was in a dangerous situation, but he also knew that he had the skills and the determination to survive.

He took a deep breath and closed his eyes, feeling the warmth of the fire spreading through his achy body. He realized that he had a long road ahead of him, but he also knew that giving up meant dying, and dying wasn't going to be on his agenda now.

Arthur laid back resting his head on his backpack as he listened to the smooth hum of the crackle of the fire in front of him. He looked up at the cracks of his shelter marveling at the night sky, seeing the star's dance with the northern lights with a poetic grace that went unmatched to anything he had seen out here.

With the fire keeping him warm, and the cold Alaskan sky over his shelter, Arthur didn't just feel one with nature, but he could feel one with God. He closed his eyes and began to pray.

"God it's me Arthur. I know it's been a while since we've last talked, and I'm pretty sure it would've been a bit longer if the last few day's hadn't happened. But as you can see I'm in quite a bind here. I'm not asking for you to save me from death, but what I'm asking is if there's hope please give me a sign. I need it now more than ever my Lord."

After Arthur finished his prayer he drifted off to sleep as the glow of the fire hugged him with a much-needed sense of comfort.

Chapter Four:

An Unexpected Partnership

A few hour's later at the crack of dawn, Arthur woke up to the sound of twigs snapping nearby. When he had opened his eyes, he was startled to see a young teenage boy, no more than fourteen years old, pointing a crossbow at him. Arthur's first instinct was to reach for his own weapon in defense, but he quickly realized that his rifle was out of reach, and he was now left defenseless.

"Hey asshole what are you doing in these woods?" the boy asked, his voice low and cautious.

Before he could reply, Arthur took a deep breath and tried to sit up, but the pain in his leg and forehead stopped him In his tracks. It was only when he had taken that brief second, and gathered his bearings he started to speak with caution. "I'm just a prepper," he replied with a groan of pain. "I was attacked by a pack of wolves and I'm resting here until I can walk again."

The boy lowered his crossbow seeing that Arthur was indeed hurt, but he didn't put it away. "You're lucky to be alive out here," he said. "The wolves around here don't usually leave survivors."

Arthur could only nod in his weakened response. "I know. I was lucky to have my rifle with me."

The boy frowned as Arthur's word's caught his attention. "Where is it?"

Arthur then pointed to the other side of his shelter with trepidation. "Over there, against the tree. I can't reach it right now, I'm in too much pain."

The boy then walked over to the rifle and picked it up, where he examined it carefully, checking the ammunition and the safety. Once he saw the weapon was out of ammo he handed it back to Arthur with mindfulness of the man's body language. "Again you're lucky I found you before something else did," he said looking around the wooden area. "There are a lot more dangerous creatures in these woods then just wolves."

Arthur looked at the boy, trying to read his expression. He was clearly wary of strangers, but there was something else in his eyes, something that Arthur couldn't quite place. "Who are you?" he asked.

The boy hesitated for a moment, then he spoke. "My name is Caleb. Caleb Cane, and I live in these woods. I have for a very long time now."

Arthur nodded in acknowledgement before introducing himself. "I'm Arthur, Arthur Peters and thank you for helping me, well not helping me, but for not killing me I suppose."

Caleb only shrugged in response. "I didn't do anything yet. And if I do it's because I just don't like the idea of someone dying in my territory. Plus I don't kill unless I have to." The teen said stern-faced as he let Arthur know he wasn't scared of the man that sat before him.

Arthur couldn't help, but smile at the boy's remarks. "Fair enough, do you know anything about survival skills? I could use some help with my injuries, I'm pretty banged up here kid."

Caleb looked at Arthur's leg and forehead, then he nodded. "I know a few things. I'll help you, but you'll have to do what I say." Arthur nodded in agreement letting the boy know that he was willing to come to terms on Caleb's conditions.

"Do you have a camp out here or something?" Arthur questioned the teen with curiosity.

"Yeah I have somewhere safe I can take you to, just don't do anything stupid, and don't act like a shit-head and we'll be good."

Arthur couldn't help but laugh at Caleb's smart mouth. "Yeah you got a deal kid, I won't do anything stupid, you have my word."

So together, they slowly made their way through the dense forest, with the boy helping to support Arthur as he hobbled along.

After what seemed like several hours of walking, and taking intermittent breaks for Arthur to rest up, they finally reached a hidden trench shelter that the young Survivor had made by himself during one of his previous adventures. The shelter was reinforced with car parts and even an old backseat, dropped with a yellow tarp with homemade stairs built from wood, making it a sturdy and secure place to rest and recover.

Inside the shelter, the boy tended to Arthur's wounds as best as he could, using supplies he had from his own emergency stash he had stored away, as well as local remedies he had learned over the year's and growing up. Despite his injuries, Arthur was grateful to have found such a safe haven, and he couldn't help but marvel at the ingenuity of the shelter's construction.

As Arthur rested up and began to recover, he shared with the boy about his experience with the pack of wolves that had nearly brought him to his death. That they had trapped him, and attempted to kill him. And that even though he was able to take down what he thought was half of the beasts, the others were still out there.

"Well that was stupid of you to run out of a fucking Cabin in the first place." Caleb said with mockery as he handed Arthur a cup of homemade tea from the fresh natural fire weeds he had stashed away.

"Yeah definitely not my brightest moment." Arthur snickered lightly to nobody in particularly, but winced from the pain it caused before taking a gentle sip of the fresh brewed liquid.

"So if I'm going to help you we need to make one thing clear. If you are staying around me you can't be making dumbass choices while I'm around, got it Mr. Survival man."

Arthur agreed, and for the next few days, he and Caleb worked together to survive in the harsh Alaskan wilderness. Caleb showed Arthur how to make a fire without his fire striker, how to find edible plants, and how to trap small game like small Grouse. All of which Arthur had already knew, but he wanted to see how much exactly the boy knew on his own.

He also helped Arthur with his injuries, cleaning and re-bandaging his wounds every day.

At first, Arthur was wary of Caleb's motives. He didn't know why a young boy would be living alone in the woods out here, and he was afraid that Caleb might be trying to soften him up so he could lead him into a trap. But that all changed one faithful crisp day.

As Arthur was out scavenging, and checking the traps he and Caleb had set in the morning he came across a terrifying moment where he came face to face with a black grizzly. It had been disturbed of it's hibernation due to the frequent activity going on outside.

Arthur was aware that these animals could run upwards to thirty miles per hour, and could rip the flesh of your body within seconds.

As the bear looked into his eyes, Arthur was ready to welcome once again the possibility of his own death. He braced himself as the beast began to make it's way in his direction.

Then suddenly a loud noise hissed the cold winter air scaring both Arthur, and the black grizzly.

When he opened his eyes, the man saw the animal was running away in terror. Arthur then changed his focus into the direction of the ear-splitting noise that had saved him. He was surprised when he saw Caleb holding an air horn towards the sky with a smile.

"Like I said dude, don't do anything stupid around me." The boy then walked up to Arthur, and proceeded to hand him a large bowie knife.

"Next time you want to leave camp make sure you're prepared." Caleb said with a chuckle before heading back to camp.

"It was an honest mistake man!" Arthur hollered out to Caleb to let him know that accidents happen.

"Mistakes get you killed, out here, Mr. Survival man!" Caleb yelled from around the corner with a cold sarcastic humor in his voice.

As the days then proceeded to go by, Arthur began to trust Caleb more and more despite his mocking approach. He realized that the boy was smart and resourceful, and that he knew these woods better than anyone else, even himself.

One night, Arthur and Caleb huddled together in their perspective corners inside the small trench shelter, trying to stay warm as they cooked their meager dinner over a small fire. They had been living in this shelter for several weeks now, and conditions were only getting worse outside as December approached them. The temperature was dropping rapidly, and any game that was available had taken shelter elsewhere to avoid the frigid cold.

While they ate, Arthur and Caleb talked about their dwindling supplies. They had only a few days worth of food left from previous catches of game, and their water supply was running low. It was reaching minus twenty degrees outside in these parts of the woods, and any risk of leaving their safe structure meant freezing to death in minutes. But Arthur knew that they would have to venture out soon, despite the danger.

Suddenly, they heard a rustling in the bushes outside of their makeshift fortress. Arthur's heart skipped a beat as he reached for his rifle, but he quickly realized once again that he had used up all of his ammunition in his previous encounter with the killer pack.

Both him and the boy were caught off guard for they had thought they were out of the wolves territory, and they had been safe. But what was awaiting them was a sign of what was only just the beginning of the next terrifying hurdle.

Caleb grabbed his crossbow, and Arthur took up his bowie knife that the teen gave him. They both knew that they had to be careful, as they feared they were outnumbered and outmatched by the packs suspected high numbers outside.

Both he and Caleb made ear-splitting screams, and hollers to make the wolves outside go in the other direction. But the familiar snarling growls, and approaching footsteps made it clear to them that these rabid hounds were not going to be backing off.

Arthur was aware from his former encounter, that the last time of the packs attack, he had barely made it out alive. And now that the survivalist was still injured he knew that the situation was going to take more than what he could do on his own. He doubted his abilities, but luckily for him he had Caleb to assist in this approaching battle. But was it going to be enough? The middle-aged man couldn't help but have the treacherous thought cross his mind.

He was taking a moment to observe the snowy grounds once they were outside, trying to get a glimpse of any sign of the wolves when suddenly they appeared out of the infinite darkness, His worst suspicions were indeed true. Their numbers were even larger than the last time. They were all lashing out and baring their teeth broadly.

Arthur and Caleb stood their ground, where they were ready to fight. The first wolf lunged at them, and Caleb let loose an arrow from his crossbow where it hit the wolf right in the chest, but it didn't slow the animal down. Arthur swung his knife, but he missed, striking the ground below instead. The wolf then leaped high behind Arthur, but was met with another arrow from Caleb who killed it.

The next few minutes were a blur of movement and noise. Caleb fired arrow after arrow, while Arthur used his knife to fend off the wolves that got too close. They managed to take down several of the animals, but more kept on coming. It seemed like a never ending fight that might lead to the duo's death. They were running on fumes at this point. Both of them were breathing harder, their body's growing stiffer from the cold blistering air that hugged them.

Their lungs burned with each attempt to inhale. The joints of their bodies cried for warmth, and rest. The combination of the battle, and mother nature's greetings were more than any human body should ever have to sustain.

All hope seemed at a loss when finally, Caleb succeeded once again with the crossbow and fired a bolt, hitting the largest wolf in the head and killing it instantly.

The remaining wolves fled in terror seeing this, and Arthur and Caleb both collapsed onto the ground, panting and exhausted. They had fought off the attack, but they knew that they were lucky to have survived. Arthur's injured leg throbbed with pain, and he knew that he needed to rest and still heal before they could try to venture out.

As they rested by the fire, recovering from the adrenaline rush from their collision with the pack, Arthur and Caleb talked about their close call. They knew that they were running low on supplies, and that they would have to face more dangers if they wanted to survive. However, they were still determined to make it through this, together.

So as a team, Arthur and Caleb battled the harsh conditions of the Alaskan winter. They fought off a few more wolves that would attempt to approach their shelter and other predators, braved blizzards and freezing temperatures, and struggled to find enough food and even risk trips to the stream for water to stay alive. But despite all the hardships, they formed a bond that was stronger than anything either of them had experienced in a long time. They became friends, relying on each other for survival in a world that was harsh and unforgiving.

One night as they were resting from a day of forging, and gathering materials the older survivalist knew that they needed to look at long term solutions about finding a way out of their predicament.

Arthur looked over at Caleb, who was huddled beside him near the fire. "Do you know of any paths that can lead you and I to civilization?" he asked.

Caleb could only shake his head somberly. "The only way out of these woods is through the territory of the pack that keeps attacking us. It's only in the direction of your cabin that you've mentioned before. I've checked, there's no other way."

Arthur frowned with slight frustration before he spoke. "But we have to try. We can't stay out here forever. We need to at least attempt to get back to the cabin we can get more supplies there." The man said with a bit of optimism Trying to replace the frustration in his voice

Caleb looked up at him, where his eyes were filled with emotion. "You don't understand." he said, "Those wolves killed my dad in the beginning of this. I've been trapped out here for six years because of them. There's no way we can risk it. If we take that risk we die! I was eight years old when my dad took me hunting out here. We slid off the road, and we hit a tree."

Caleb then took a deep breath before continuing between his sobs. "I can still remember the way his blood felt on my hands. I realized that there was this loud pitch noise blaring. It hurt my ears, it wasn't until later on I realized it was my very own screams. I was screaming from the sight of the tree branch shoving into my dad's chest."

The boy stared blankly into space before taking a minute before he carried on. "Later after I ran away scared, and I found a tunnel. It was that night I heard the wolves fighting one another. I kept wondering to myself what it was they were attacking each other for. It was only the next day when I went back to get the stuff for the shelter I realized they were fighting over his body."

Caleb sat looking at the fire as he spoke. "These clothes I'm wearing are the clothes he had packed for himself for our trip. It's all I could gather. As I was now in their territory. I took parts from the truck one day where I saw what was left of my dad's body. I also stripped additional materials from the front seat as much as I could, and dragged it back to this spot. I tried going back a third time, but the wolves chased me and I haven't been back since."

Arthur was taken aback by Caleb's revelation. He had no idea that the boy had been living in the woods for so long, let alone that he had lost his father to the very creatures they were trying to avoid. "I'm so sorry kid" he said. "I had no idea."

Caleb wiped away the tears that were now beginning to form in his eyes. "It's okay," he said trying to pull himself together. "I've learned to survive out here. But I can't go through that territory again. It's just too dangerous. Every time I've ever tried, they come for me. They have me out numbered. What we've seen is nothing, because over there it might as well be an army of them."

Arthur hesitated for a moment before speaking. "I understand how you feel, but we have to take the risk. We can't stay out here forever, and we can't survive much longer without proper shelter and supplies. We have to at least try to do this kid."

Caleb looked at Arthur, his eyes filled with a mixture of fear and anger. "You don't understand," he said. "You don't know what it's like to lose someone you love to those wolves. You don't know what it's like to be trapped out here for years, with no way out. You don't know anything!"

Arthur reached out and put a hand on Caleb's shoulder. "I may not know what you've been through, but I do know that we're in this together. We have to rely on each other if we want to survive. Please Caleb, think about it, we can do this as a team."

Caleb looked down at the ground, his shoulders slumped as his emotions conflicted with his skills that already lay within him. For a few moments, there was only the sound of the fire crackling in the background. Then, Caleb looked up at Arthur with a frustrated expression on his face. "No," he said. "We'll die if we do."

"Caleb please I'm begging you I can't do this alone." Arthur said pleading for the boy to come around.

"No!" Caleb shouted before getting up, and walking out already angered by Arthur's persistence.

Arthur waited a few minutes giving the young survivor, time to get his thoughts together before trying again. He knew that they both needed to wrap their minds around their current situation.

It wasn't easy, but he knew they needed to try. If they could somehow make it to Arthur's cabin he knew they had a shot at surviving.

After several minutes Arthur stood up, and walked to peak his head outside to make sure the boy was okay. When he saw that Caleb was nowhere to be found he called out his name to make sure the boy was within ear shot distance.

But all that came in response was the heavy cry of the wind blowing. A blizzard decided to hit only moments later after Caleb had left. Now the gravity of Caleb's circumstances fell on Arthur's shoulders.

The boy was lost In this, and he had no way of finding his way back to camp. Arthur had no choice now, he had to set out to find him no matter the cost.

Chapter Five:

The Search Begins

Arthur looked around as he heard the sound of snow hitting the tarp above him. He stood there and rubbed his eyes from exhaustion, trying to shake off the grogginess from this already long treacherous night. He had been searching for Caleb for a few hour's, but he wasn't sure where the boy had gone. The blizzard had made the landscape unrecognizable, and he couldn't see more than a few feet in front of him. He knew that he would need to start his search again soon, but before he did, he was aware that he had to make a makeshift blanket from one of the wolves that the pair had killed.

Even though Arthur was a seasoned survivalist, he knew that the blizzard outside was going to make his task all the more difficult.

Arthur was mindful that he had to find Caleb before the blizzard got any worse more than it already had, but he also knew that he needed to make use of the wolf hide. The hide would provide Caleb with much-needed warmth and protection from the elements outside. Arthur understood that hypothermia was going to be a risk out here for the boy, and time was of the essence.

He quickly got to work, using his bowie knife to carefully skin the wolfs corpse. He worked like lightning, knowing that time was becoming more crucial with each second. As he worked, he couldn't help but think about Caleb and the danger that he was now in. He silently prayed that the teenager had managed to find some form of shelter from the blizzard.

Once he had finished skinning the wolf, Arthur set to work tanning the hide over the fire. He perceived that this was going to be a time-consuming process, but he also knew that it was necessary. He had to make sure that the hide was properly tanned if he wanted it to provide Caleb with any real protection.

While he worked, the blizzard outside continued to rage. The wind howled, and snow piled up against the outside walls of the small trench shelter. He knew that he had to finish making the hide and find Caleb before it was too late.

Finally, after what seemed like hours, the hide was ready. Arthur quickly wrapped it up and put it in his bag. He was determined to begin his deepened search.

Arthur wanted to start by retracing their steps from the previous day, but was aware the heavy snow falling would make it a near impossible challenge. He gathered more of his gear, strapped on his heavy snowshoes once more, and stepped out of the shelter. The wind was singing loudly, and the snow was coming down hard, making it difficult for him to keep his balance. He followed the memories of their tracks from the day before, but he wasn't sure due to the fact that their footprints were now covered up by the heavy snow.

As he walked, and he left markings to follow on his way back to camp, Arthur called out Caleb's name like before, but he was met with only the sound of the unforgiving wind again. He felt a pang of guilt, knowing that he should have been more understanding of Caleb's reluctance to leave. He had been so focused on survival that he hadn't realized what it was like to be a scared teenager who went through such trauma.

He pushed those thoughts aside and focused on the task at hand. He wandered through the blizzard for what seemed like hours, but was only thirty minutes. Thirty long grueling minutes of zigzagging through the dense Alaskan forest, trying to find any sign of Caleb. He found nothing but more snow and silence.

As the night wore on, Arthur's energy started to wane. He had brought the little food, tea and water they had at camp, but he understood that he needed to find Caleb soon. The blizzard showed no signs of letting up, and he didn't want to risk getting lost in this storm himself.

Just as he was about to admit his defeat, he saw something in the distance. It was a flash of red, and it caught his attention immediately. He trudged through the deep snow towards it, hoping that it was a sign of Caleb.

When he got closer, Arthur realized that it was a red backpack. He recognized it immediately as Caleb's. He felt a surge of relief mixed with dread. He knew that Caleb wouldn't have left his backpack behind willingly. It meant that something had happened to him.

Arthur searched the area around the backpack frantically, calling out Caleb's name again and again. He scoured the space for any clues, but he found nothing. It was as if Caleb had vanished into thin air.

The survivalists heart sank as he realized that he was completely lost in his search for his friend. He had no idea where to go from here. He was in the middle of this harsh blizzard, with little to no food or water, and the supplies he had already brought along he wanted to save for Caleb. He had no idea where the teen was. So, relying on his faith he sat down in the snow and closed his eyes and took a deep breath, trying to calm himself down. He knew that panicking wouldn't help him find the youngster. He had to stay concentrated and come up with a plan of action.

When he opened his eyes, Arthur had a new found sense of calmness and looked around, trying to get his bearings. He was grateful as he took notice of a tree with a broken branch nearby in the distance. He remembered passing by it earlier in the previous day's as he had forged through the landscape. He quickly stood up and walked towards the tree, his snowshoes meeting the white sheets of the uncontrolled snow.

When he reached the large trunk, he broke off a peace of the branch and held it up, where he was able to begin examining it closely. He noticed that the bark had been scraped off in a few places, revealing the lighter wood underneath.

"Maybe Caleb did this." Arthur said as he thought to himself. "Maybe he was trying to leave me a sign."

He looked around and saw more trees with similar markings. He realized that they formed a trail leading away from where he had found Caleb's backpack.

Arthur's heart raced as he now followed the mysterious puzzle, his mind filled with a mix of hope and fear. He didn't know what he would find at the end of the series of these markings, but he knew that he had to follow it.

As he walked, he noticed that the trail was getting fainter. The snow was coming down even harder with mother nature laughing at his very soul taunting him, covering up the markings on the trees. He started to panic, wondering if he had lost the only clue he had been given.

"Come on, Caleb," he whispered. "Don't give up on me now kid."

Suddenly, he heard a faint sound in the background of the storms raging winds. It was a voice, and it sounded like Caleb's. Arthur's head quickly shot up, ignoring the growing pain in his stiff joints, and started running towards the sound.

He ran as fast as he could, following the low echoes of Caleb's voice. He could barely see anything in the blizzard, but he didn't care. He was determined to find his friend.

After what felt like a pause in time itself, and being stuck in a phase of panic, he finally saw a figure up ahead. It was indeed Caleb, stumbling towards him through the snow, looking exhausted and terrified. Arthur ran towards him with desperation. Seeing his friend already knocking at heaven's gates with death looming over his shoulder, behind him was a sight that Arthur would never forget.

As Arthur approached Caleb, he could see that his friend was without question in dire shape. His lips were blue, his skin was pale, and his breathing was very shallow. He couldn't speak from being so weak already. Caleb only had a glazed look over his face that was haunting to see. Arthur knew that he had to act fast to prevent the teen stricken with broken blood vessels from slipping into hypothermia further.

Arthur quickly assessed the situation and realized that the first thing they needed was shelter. He looked around and spotted a small grove of trees a few hundred yards away with squinted vision. He guided Caleb towards the hidden lifesaving evergreen, all the while shouting encouraging words to keep him conscious.

Once they reached the grove, Arthur started gathering materials to build a shelter. He found some fallen branches and started arranging them into a teepee-like structure. The man then covered the branches with pine needles and leaves to create a thick layer of insulation.

As he worked, Arthur noticed that Caleb's glazed look had turned into a vacant stare now. He knew that he had to act quickly, so he dragged Caleb into the shelter and started a fire.

Arthur was glad he had brought some kindling and his fire striker with him, so starting the fire was easy. Once it was going, he placed Caleb as close to the fire as possible without burning him. Arthur then removed Caleb's frozen clothes and wrapped him in the wolf hide he had made, and stored away in his own backpack.

As he worked, Arthur kept talking to Caleb, trying to keep him conscious and alert. He knew that hypothermia could cause confusion and disorientation, and he didn't want Caleb to slip into a coma. The boy was already exhibiting symptoms of stage two hypothermia when Arthur had found him, and was quickly approaching stage three.

But the survivalist was hell-bent on making sure the boy would live. Arthur wasn't going to lose the only friend he had, not when he already had lost so much in the past. So, the man did the one last thing in his arsenal of skill he knew of that he could do as a last resort. Getting ready he started rubbing the boy's chest roughly, before starting small chest compressions to circulate the blood in Caleb's body.

But just as Arthur had started, things quickly became worse as Caleb's frozen stiff body, went limp with despair.

Arthur's heart raced as he hurriedly leaned over his friend, who now lay there motionless on the cold ground in front of him. The biting wind's wrapping their way around their makeshift shelter presently, had threatened to numb their bodies before, were now a mere cry of God who wept over the pair's circumstances, but Arthur's determination burned hotter than ever. As he worked with still trembling hands, he pressed down harder on Caleb's chest with desperation, performing the compressions, desperately trying to revive him.

"Come on, Caleb! Stay with me!" Arthur's voice cracked with raw emotion; his words laced with urgency. "You can't give up! Fight kid, damn it!" The man said just as he saw Caleb's eyes roll up into his young skull.

Caleb's pale face now displayed the effects of his impending death, his lips still tinged with a bluish hue. The freezing temperatures had now taken their toll, threatening to steal away his young life. But Arthur refused to let that happen. He refused to lose his friend.

The panic in Arthur's voice reverberated through the desolate landscape of their shelter. "Wake up, Caleb! Breathe! You're not allowed to leave me here alone!"

With each compression, Arthur poured every ounce of his strength into Caleb's now lifeless body, praying for a response. The tension in the air was palpable, the weight of the situation pressing heavily on Arthur's shoulders.

"Don't you dare give up on me, Caleb!" Arthur's voice became a desperate plea, his words punctuated by the rhythm of his compressions. "We've been through too much together now. We aren't supposed to make dumbass decisions kid. Remember!"

As the seconds ticked by, hope seemed to dwindle, but Arthur refused to surrender. Beads of sweat trickled down his forehead, mixing with the frigid tears that streamed down his cheeks. The effort was physically and emotionally draining, but he couldn't afford to let go.

"You're stronger than this, kid!" Arthur's voice cracked; his voice hoarse from strained exertion. "I won't let you slip away. Fight back, damn it! Fight for your life Caleb!"

Suddenly, a faint gasp escaped Caleb's lips, as if a spark of life had reignited within him. Arthur's heart leaped with renewed hope, fueling his determination to keep going.

"That's it, Caleb! Breathe! Stay with me, buddy!" Arthur's voice trembled with equal parts relief and anxiety. "I'm right here, fighting beside you. You're not alone in this!"

With each passing second, Caleb's gasps grew stronger, his chest rising and falling in irregular rhythms. Arthur's hands shook as he continued the compressions, his voice filled with a mix of desperation and reassurance.

"Just a little bit more, Caleb! Hold on!" Arthur's voice quivered with emotion. "I won't let you go. Not now. Not ever, kid!"

Sure, enough after several minutes, Caleb started to shiver and his color started to return. Arthur remembered that this was a good sign and stopped his compressions. But still he continued to monitor him closely with his anxiety at an all-time high. He made sure that Caleb stayed warm and hydrated, giving him small sips of Caleb's fire weed tea that Arthur brought from the trench shelter and storing it in his water bottle. The boy would barely respond to the warm fluids meeting his lips, but still tried in his weakened state.

As the night wore on, the blizzard had only intensified. The wind sang it's way through the trees, and the snow piled up outside the shelter. But inside, Arthur and Caleb were now warm and safe.

Arthur was falling asleep as the length of his exhaustion started to set in. His head slowly dropping meeting his folded arm's

"So you found me." Caleb said with a hint of humor, and a weakness in his voice as he finally was able to speak. This action caused his friend to snap back to reality, and respond.

"I had to, I wanted to remind you again, that we aren't supposed to make dumbass decisions, remember." Arthur said with a light chuckle.

"Thank you man, I didn't know how much longer I was going to last. I was so frustrated I didn't realize how far I walked until it got worse." Caleb said as he rubbed the sleep out his eye's.

"Still that was pretty fucking stupid of you to run out in a blizzard." Arthur said mockingly which made Caleb laugh in return.

"Yeah that was pretty stupid. I guess that talking about everything just was too much for me. I miss him so much,

Arthur." The boy said in a somber tone as he once again recalled the memory of his dead father.

"I know how you feel kid. Trust me I know." Arthur said softly trying to reassure the boy.

"Yeah, and how do you know that feeling?" Caleb said with his head turning to Arthur's direction now.

"Before I started this whole survival skill thing. I had it all at a young age. A job, a wife, and a son. One day, me and my wife Zoey we wanted to take a vacation up here from Seattle." Arthur paused taking a minute before beginning the origins of his haunting past.

"When we were about halfway up the trip, we were struck by a drunk driver. I didn't realize I hadn't buckled our son Nicholas in properly. My wife I just remember her singing along to the radio. I sang with her, and when I turned to look at her, I just saw headlights. When I woke up both my wife, and son were dead." Arthur giving his turn to stare at the fire as he was speaking.

"My job at the bank I worked at couldn't wait for me very long. So after a while I lost it, and just gave up. Pretty much after that I sold my house, and took my savings and learned to survive off different lands."

"Arthur I didn't know I'm so sorry." Caleb said having his turn to sympathize with his friend.

"Don't be, but after a while my best friend became Johnnie Walker. When that happened I had planned one night where I was going to have a good meal, with a bottle and just end it all. I was having that meal when the wolves showed up."

Caleb nodded slowly understanding the gravity of the ordeal Arthur had been through.

"I guess the whole thing with these wolves was a blessing, because it showed me how much I wanted to live. And I also gained a best friend out of it." Arthur said as the pair fist-bumped one another.

That night they realized something they weren't just friends, but they were brothers.

In the morning, the blizzard had passed, and the sun was shining. Arthur knew that they had to make their way back to camp soon, but he also was aware that Caleb was in no condition to travel back to the trench shelter. So, he decided to stay put for another few days to give Caleb time to recover.

During that time, Arthur took care of Caleb, making sure he was warm, hydrated, and well-fed with what they had. He also kept a close eye on him, monitoring his vital signs and looking for any signs of infection or other complications due to the scare they had been through.

Later that same afternoon Caleb sat up, and decided to clear the air with Arthur further.

"Hey Arthur can I tell you something." Caleb said lightly.

"Sure kid what's up, are you feeling okay?" Arthur questioned with concern.

"Yeah I'm fine I just, I just wanted to know if you were still interested in trying to get out of here." Caleb said looking at Arthur with a serious expression.

Arthur nodded listening to the boy, and followed by adding a simple. "Yeah."

"What if we got back to camp, and figure out a plan to get closer to the cabin you came from without becoming discovered by the wolves." Caleb suggested with a bit enthusiasm.

"You seem strong enough, if you feel like you are ready, we'll go back in the morning. After we reach camp, we'll figure out a plan. Arthur replied with a smile.

"Okay it sounds like it's settled then. In the morning we'll make our way back to camp." Caleb said with cheer.

Chapter Six:

The Journey To The Cabin

Arthur and Caleb set out from their temporary shelter, and were trudging through the deep snow that had accumulated during the blizzard. The wind had died down, but the cold still bit at their faces and hands. They had to keep moving to stay warm.

Caleb was feeling much better after the hypothermia scare, but he was still weak and his movements were unhurried and unsteady. Arthur knew they had to take it slow and cautious if they wanted to get back to their camp safely.

Now that the blizzard had been over, and it had been a few days, the pair were able to see they were able to follow the path that Arthur had marked on his way out of the trench shelter to where they currently were. But the snow had still covered most of his tracks, making it difficult to find their way back to camp.

But still Arthur led the way, using his vast knowledge, and survival skills to navigate through the wilderness using everything he knew from the paths of the wind too the direction of the sun.

As they walked, Arthur and Caleb talked about their plan to reach the safe haven of the cabin without running into any of the wolves. Arthur explained that they needed to avoid open areas where the wolves could easily spot them and stick to the trees where they could move quietly and remain hidden. He also advised Caleb to stay close and to keep his wits about him.

While Arthur and Caleb trudged through the thick white underbrush, their boots were sinking into the snowy grounds with each step. They took note of the snow that had been relentless in the last few days, turning the forest into a soggy mess. But that didn't dampen their spirits. They were survivors, after all, and a little snow was nothing compared to the bond they had built together as a team.

"So, Caleb, you think we'll make it back to camp before the sun sets?" Arthur asked, wiping the slight frost that was beginning to form on his brow.

Caleb smirked as he adjusted his backpack. "Oh, definitely. We'll be back in our cozy trench shelter, sipping hot tea and roasting wild grouse by the fireplace in no time."

Arthur raised an eyebrow before responding to the boy. "That's a vivid imagination you have there. But hey, as long as we don't encounter that man-eating black grizzly bear, I came in contact with that one time, So I think I'm game."

Caleb chuckled hearing Arthur's words. "Right, because black grizzly bears are known for their impeccable manners. 'Excuse me, sir, do you mind if I devour you for dinner?'"

They both burst into laughter, the sound echoing through the trees. The light snow seemed to lighten more, as if even mother nature was amused by their banter.

As they plodded on, Arthur's eyes scanned the surroundings, always alert. He noticed a broken branch poking out of the bushes up ahead. "Hey, Caleb, check out that branch. Looks like something big passed through here recently."

Caleb rolled his eyes. "Oh, you mean your mother, just kidding but come on Arthur. It's probably just a squirrel on fucking steroids. Can we focus on our imaginary grizzly bears instead?"

Arthur smirked. "You know what they say, kid. Ignorance is bliss until a squirrel on steroids comes crashing through your fucking window."

Caleb chuckled nervously. "Alright, alright, point taken. I'll keep an eye out for killer squirrels. Happy now?"

"Ecstatic," Arthur replied, grinning. "But seriously, let's stay alert here. We've survived this long because we pay attention to the little things that others might miss."

They continued their journey, the snow gradually tapering off. Their conversation was a mix of sarcastic humor and genuine concern for each other's well-being. They shared stories of their previous adventures of survival, exaggerating the details for comedic effect.

Suddenly, Arthur's keen eyes caught sight of a peculiar shadow hovering over a nearby tree. He stopped in his tracks, his heart now beginning to pound.

"What's up, Mr. survivor man?" Caleb asked, noticing Arthur's sudden change in demeanor.

Arthur pointed at the tree cautiously. "Look there, kid. Something's not right. That shadow, it's moving."

Caleb squinted, his face turning serious. "You think it's another squirrel on steroids?"

Arthur scowled playfully. "Very fucking funny, wise guy. But no, this feels different. We need to be cautious here."

They approached the tree carefully, their survival instincts kicking into high gear now. As they drew closer, a snow owl unexpectedly burst out from the branches, startling them both.

Arthur let out a relieved laugh. "Well, would you look at that? It was just an owl. Talk about anticlimactic."

Caleb grinned sheepishly. "Hey, at least it wasn't a squirrel on steroids."

They both burst into laughter once again, their worries forgotten in the joy of the moment.

Soon after their owl scare, they approached a clearing a few yards up. Things had seemed to be on track when Arthur stopped momentarily, and signaled for Caleb to stop in his tracks. He could hear something moving in the snow up ahead. They hunched down behind a fallen log and waited. And sure enough after those few tense growing moments, they saw the dangerous pack of wolves instantaneously emerge from the trees on the other side of the clearing. They knew the games were over, and it was time to face reality of their situation once more.

Arthur being quick on his feet told Caleb to stay on the ground and hide behind the log. He was whispering for the teen to stay quiet and as still as possible. The wolves stood there as they sniffed the air, before they explored the area looking for more prey, and then suddenly began to move in the direction of the hidden duo. Arthur slowly reached for his knife, ready to defend himself and Caleb, if necessary, but the odds of him fending off the wolves on his own was a suicide mission.

The frigid wind still howled through the dense forest, carrying with it a chilling sense of foreboding. Arthur and Caleb kept crouching behind the dead fallen log, their breaths still visible in the icy air. The snow-covered ground beneath them trembled with each approaching thud of the heavy paws that drew closer, and closer. They knew they were currently trapped, surrounded by this pack of merciless beasts.

Arthur's heart wanted to explode in his chest, his senses heightened to every sound, and every movement. His hands kept shaking involuntarily, a mixture of fear and adrenaline coursing through his middle-aged veins. He cast a quick glance at Caleb, whose face was pale and sweat-drenched, but not from mother nature this time. But his eyes wide with terror as he knew the murderous hounds were meters away from them.

The wolves 'eerie howls pulsated through the silent daylight, sending shivers down the spines of the two survivors. The vibrations of the wolves' harmonious tunes suddenly seemed to come from all directions, making it impossible to discern how many of the predators were truly there. Their glowing eyes flickered in the shadows of the tree's dancing with the sun, their predatory gaze fixated on the scent of the prey hiding just beyond their reach.

The scent of blood hung heavily in the air, a sinister reminder of the wolves' hunger. Arthur's mind raced, desperately seeking a way out of their perilous situation. But as the pack closed in even deeper, their options dwindled. They were outnumbered, outmatched, and now trapped again in a deadly game of survival.

A sudden snap of a twig shattered the silence, freezing the duo in their tracks. The wolves paused, their heads turning in unison toward the source of the noise. Time seemed to crawl as Arthur and Caleb held their breath, praying that whatever had made the sound would divert the wolves' attention away from them.

But their hopes were shattered when the wolves' piercing snarls echoed again and again through the forest. The predators had finally caught their scent. Their primal instincts helped them navigate forward, due to the hunger fueling their relentless pursuit. The two survivor's worst nightmare was now unfolding before their very own eyes.

With each passing second, the wolves closed in, their predatory growls growing louder and more menacing. Arthur's mind raced, searching for any shred of hope. Desperation clouded his thoughts as he considered his options. Fight or flight? But how could they fight a pack of wolves armed with nothing but their own trembling bodies, and one bowie knife? And flight seemed impossible, as the wolves had already seemed to surround them, cutting off any possible escape route for the time being.

Fear consumed Arthur and Caleb, their bodies trembling uncontrollably from both the cold, and terror. The wolves' eyes glinted in the middle of the Alaskan day as they drew nearer, their breath visible like the two survivors' breath in the cold air as well. Time was running out. The men exchanged a final, knowing glance, silently acknowledging the grim fate that awaited them.

As the wolves were about to close in, their snarls growing deafening, Arthur and Caleb braced themselves for the inevitable. In the face of imminent danger, they held on to a flicker of hope, a desperate belief that perhaps, somehow, they might outwit the relentless hunters. But deep down, they knew that survival in this cruel and unforgiving wilderness was a mere illusion, and the only certainty that awaited them was the horrifying jaws of the relentless pack.

But just as the wolves were about to pounce, and all hope was lost, they heard a loud glunking in the distance, and the vicious animals hearing this sound quickly jumped at the opportunity, suddenly turning and ran swiftly back into the forest. Arthur and Caleb breathed a deep sigh of relief and felt a wave of emotion release as they had dodged their biggest bullet yet.

However, they couldn't rest now, and needed to continue on their way back to their sanctuary where they could gather themselves.

When they made sure the coast was indeed clear, they started their route again and walked further, and sure enough after what only could've been an hours more walk on the pairs internal clock, they were relieved to finally see the trench shelter in the far off distance. They hurriedly quickened their pace, eager to get warm and dry.

When they arrived, they found their shelter intact, but they needed to start a fire, and Arthur quickly got to work, gathering more firewood and using his fire striker to get it going. Once it was done Caleb sat by the flames, warming his hands and feet.

After a while of recuperating, Arthur and Caleb began to discuss their next move. They knew they couldn't stay at the shelter forever, but they needed a plan properly to get to Arthur's cabin safely. They decided to wait until morning, when the light would help them navigate through the woods like it did before.

As they settled in for the night, Arthur thought about how lucky they had been to survive the blizzard and avoid any serious harm from the wolves. He knew that their journey was far from over, but he felt confident that they could make it to his cabin together.

"If we continue to cover our tracks, and move with caution it'll help make thing's harder for them to track us." Arthur told Caleb as they began discussing the formation of their plan.

"We can always mask our scent with something. I know there's Sitka deer out here. That glunking we heard was one of them. They are the only animals that can make that sound in these woods. Maybe we can find one tomorrow, and harvest it's bladder." Caleb suggested as they both deliberated on what the best course of action could be.

"You know that could very well work kid." Arthur said in agreement.

After further discussion, Arthur and Caleb decided that it was indeed their best bet to hunt a deer with Caleb's crossbow and to harvest the bladder to use the urine to mask their scent. They knew that this was not going to be an easy task, but they were determined to do whatever it took to survive.

The next morning, they set out into the wilderness in search of the Sitka deer. Their current predicament was now dire. The wolves had picked up their scent and had been shadowing them since the previous day, making stealthy, calculated moves to wear down their prey. Arthur realized that their only hope for survival was to mask their scent, and for that, they needed the bladder of this Sitka deer.

Sitka deer, elusive and fast-moving, were known for their ability to evade predators in the dense Alaskan forests. The chemical composition of their urine acted as a natural camouflage, masking the scent of other animals and providing an effective deterrent against predators. The pair moved silently through the snow, their senses heightened as they scanned their surroundings for any sign of the elusive deer.

Arthur, ever the mentor, whispered instructions and pointers to Caleb as they crept through the snowy winter underbrush. The teenager, though a bit nervous, continued to display a growing aptitude for the hunter's craft under Arthur's guidance.

Then after a few hours of tracking it, they finally came across a young buck. Caleb quickly took aim with his crossbow and fired. The bolt which struck the deer in the chest, and then fell to the ground was a victory the pair needed, and they both fist-bumped in celebration.

Arthur and Caleb quickly approached the deer and began to harvest the bladder. It was a messy and unpleasant task, for them both but they knew it was necessary. Once they had collected enough urine, they carefully poured it over themselves and their gear, making sure to cover every inch of their bodies.

Followed by the success of their hunt, they made their way back to their shelter, and together they could hear the wolves howling in the distance. But this time, they were not afraid. They knew that they had taken the necessary steps to mask their scent and protect themselves from the untamed beasts.

When they arrived back at their shelter, they settled in for the night, feeling confident and prepared. As they lay there, listening to the wolves howl in the distance, they knew that they had done everything they could to ensure their survival. And they were ready for whatever challenges the wilderness might throw their way.

"Do you think we'll make it to the Cabin." Caleb asked Arthur as they both sat in front of the roaring fire that laid in front of them.

"Yeah I do, and not only do I think we'll make it there, but I know we'll make it out of this alive." Arthur said confidently.

"How do you know?" Caleb questioned as he looked at his older friend.

"Sometimes you just need to have faith Kid." Arthur said as he sipped his water looking at the ground.

"What's faith?" Caleb asked Arthur with curiosity, and wonder.

"Faith is what keeps you going, even when you don't feel like you can anymore. It's what makes us who we are, even if we don't believe it ourselves. Sometimes it can even be the thing that separates us from life, and death. Arthur said with a sympathetic tone in his voice.

"Arthur, do you think I have faith." Caleb asked with curiosity that only a kid his age could.

"Yeah, kid one thing's for certain you have a lot of faith." Arthur said nodding to let the boy know he was serious as he spoke his word's of wisdom.

"Thanks man that really means a lot." Caleb said with a soft smile.

"You don't need to thank me; you want to know how you really thank me kid?" Arthur asked while he began adding some more dry branches to the fire.

"How?" Caleb asked wondering what the elder had to say.

"Survive, that's how you thank me. You survive through this, through everything coming our way. You just survive it all, do you understand me." Arthur said with growing determination in his voice.

Caleb couldn't reply as the gravity of Arthur's words sank into the boy's soul. So, he just nodded in agreement.

"Okay that's enough chatting we better get some shut eye before our journey in the morning." Arthur said as he rested his head on his backpack as a makeshift pillow.

"Sounds good, goodnight, Arthur." Caleb said before falling into his own slumber.

"Yeah, goodnight kid." Arthur said as he crossed his arms thinking ahead of their journey. It would seem impossible to some, but he believed it wasn't going to be impossible for the boy. He knew that he would survive no matter what.

It was in the morning Arthur and Caleb gathered their gear and made sure to leave nothing behind that could give away their location. They recognized that the wolves had shown they had keen senses and they still needed to be as stealthy as possible if they were going to make it to Arthur's cabin. Yes, they had the masking scent of the urine, but they needed to remain focused, and ready no matter what.

Together as they stepped out of the shelter, they could still hear the distant howls of the wolves. The sound made their blood run cold every time, but they knew they had to keep moving. Arthur took the lead with his bowie knife at the ready, while Caleb followed close behind with his crossbow in his hands.

They carefully made their way through the snowy woods, trying to step as lightly as possible to avoid leaving any of their tracks for the pack that was still on their minds. Even though Arthur, and Caleb knew the area well and were able to guide themselves through the dense forest without getting lost now, their minds never lost sight of the dangers that hovered over them.

As they continued to walk their way through the snowy woods, their boots softly crunching the snow so their tracks still becoming faint and undetected. They were both semi relived to be covered in the deer urine now, as both of them knew that it was their only chance of going undetected from the pack that was still lurking.

As they walked further, they saw the sky grew darker and the wind had picked up. They could feel the temperature dropping, and they knew that a storm was coming. Suddenly, the first drops of rain began to fall, quickly turning into a downpour. It was a blow of dread not only to their situation, but to both their minds. The pair knew that rain was something they couldn't afford right now.

The rain was cold and heavy, soaking through their clothes and washing away the deer urine they had worked so tirelessly to attain. Arthur and Caleb realized with growing horror that their scent was now exposed, and the wolves would be able to track them easily.

They quickened their pace, but it was too late. They could hear the distant howling of the wolves, growing closer with every passing moment. Arthur and Caleb were fully aware that they had to find shelter, and find it fast.

After a while of running they spotted the same cave in the distance that Arthur had took refuge in before, and ran towards it, hoping it would provide them with some form of protection from the hellish animals. As they entered the cave, they saw that it was dark and cold, but it was better than being outside in the open.

"Damn it all," Arthur muttered, his voice low and tense. "We were so close to the cabin. Now we're stuck in this fucking cave, waiting for those damn things to give up."

Caleb didn't respond, but Arthur could sense his unease. The teen was still young and felt less experienced, and Arthur knew he was putting a lot of trust in him by partnering along on what seemed to be this never-ending journey.

But there was no time for doubts or second-guessing now. Arthur had to stay focused on the immediate threat at hand. He peered into the darkness of the cave, trying to get his bearings and figure out what their next move should be.

Suddenly without warning, Arthur heard a low growl from outside the cave, and his heart skipped a beat. The wolves were out there, and they were getting closer by the second.

Arthur drew his trusty knife again and held it tightly, ready to defend himself and Caleb, if necessary, like he had always done. He knew they were in a dangerous situation still, but he refused to give up or surrender.

"We'll get through this," he said, his voice firm and resolute. "We'll make it to that cabin, no matter what it takes."

Before Caleb could respond to the man's statement, Arthur walked past him already having enough with these beasts.

The grizzled middle-aged man found himself standing tall at the entrance of the cave, his bowie knife drawn and ready for a fight. In the distance, he could see one of the wolves staring back at him, but the animal didn't approach. Instead, it seemed frightened for some reason, as if it could sense the danger that lurked within the dark cave behind Arthur, or maybe it was afraid of the deadly stare, he was giving it.

Arthur knew that he had to be cautious. From everything he and Caleb had been through thus far, but this particular wolf seemed hesitant and uncertain. Perhaps it had encountered something dangerous in the cave or in the woods before and was now wary of venturing too close.

With his knife still at the ready, Arthur took a few careful steps forward, keeping his eyes on the wolf the whole time. He let the rain fall onto him as he stayed primed for a fight.

"Is everything okay?" Caleb questioned from behind.

"Yeah it seems they aren't coming any closer. We're good for now. Arthur called back.

"We should stay here for a bit, and still wait a while." Caleb said looking at his friend with a bit more caution in his voice.

"Yeah, maybe you're right kid. We'll stay put here for a while." The older survivalist said reluctantly as he backed his way back into the cold darkened cave.

He watched the animals, and their glowing eye's back their way into the forest with frustration.

Arthur knew he couldn't turn a blind eye to these hounds of evil, so he kept his focus on the woods outside as best as he could.

After a while Arthur and Caleb huddled together, trying to stay warm and dry as they waited for the storm to pass. They could hear the blood thirsty hounds howling outside, getting louder throughout the night, reminding them of their sinister presence.

As They listened to the eerie howls of the pack deep within the forest, they knew their guard couldn't wind down anytime soon.

Then without warning suddenly, they heard a loud growling noise coming from inside the cave. They realized at that moment with horror that they were not alone. The large black grizzly bear that Caleb had scared off to save Arthur prior decided to show its face once more. It had gone back to hibernating in its cave, and they had disturbed it from their sounds once again.

Arthur and Caleb knew that they were in even greater danger than ever before. They had to act fast if they were going to even have the slightest chance to survive. Arthur redrew his bowie knife, while Caleb readied his crossbow.

The black bear charged at them at a ultrahigh velocity, but Arthur and Caleb were standing their ground prepared for what the monster could give them. They fought with all their might, their weapons glinting in the dim light of the cave.

The bear was relentless and took this opportunity to swing its gigantic paw, striking Arthur right in the chest. This near fatal blow caused the older survivalist to land hard on the ground with a dramatic thud.

Caleb began at that moment to shoot multiple arrows at the unstoppable beast. But it only angered it in return. It whirled around, and charged towards him at a high speed that went into the comparison of an eighteen-wheeler truck fueled on the sole purpose of the need to kill.

Arthur looked up, and seeing his friend in danger, and took this time as an advantage, and reached for his knife, which he saw when the flickering of the reflection of its blade caught his sight. it was right at his side on the ground begging to be used. So as the bear drew even closer to his teen partner, he quickly jumped in front of Caleb without thinking, and braced for impact sacrificing himself in the process.

With lightning-fast reflexes, Arthur lunged forward and plunged his knife deep into the bear's side, just as it was about to pounce on the man's body.

Time seemed to slow down as the knife pierced through the bear's thick black fur and sank into its flesh. The sound of tearing flesh and the bear's guttural roar filled the air, mingling with Arthur's own primal scream of exertion. The weight of the beast bore down on him, pressing him further into the open air causing the man to hold up the monster's immense body.

Arthur's mind raced with a mix of horror and determination. He knew he had to hold on, to keep fighting with every ounce of his being. The bear's roars of pain reverberated through the cave, echoing off the stone walls, as its life force slowly drained away. The bear's eyes, once fierce with anger, now held a glimmer of desperation and agony.

Struggling to breathe under the weight of the bear, Arthur felt the warmth of the animal's blood seeping over his hands that clutched the hilt of the knife. The bear's muscles twitched and convulsed, its movements growing weaker with each passing moment. Arthur's body trembled with exhaustion and the strain of maintaining his grip on the knife.

Despite the intense pain and danger, Arthur's resolve remained unbroken. His eyes locked with the fading gaze of the bear, and in that moment, he felt a profound connection to the creature he had been forced to confront. He understood the bear's struggle, its instinct to survive, and their shared vulnerability in this battle for life.

As the bear's strength waned, its roars turned into pitiful whimpers, until finally, the cave fell silent. Arthur's heart was heavy with a mix of triumph and sorrow. He had survived with Caleb, but at the cost of another living being's life. The weight of the bear falling to the man's side

Afterwards both exhausted and shaken, Arthur and Caleb collapsed on the cave floor as well, trying their best to catch their breath. They knew that they were lucky to be alive, but they also knew that they had to keep moving if they were going to make it out of these woods that kept on tempting their lives with death.

"Arthur, are you okay? We need to get out of here!" Caleb said in between huffs trying to catch his breath.

"I don't think so, I can't move. Something's wrong." The man said as he had tried to sit up, but was halted by a searing pain coursing its way through his body.

"Here let me take a look." Caleb said, getting up and approaching his friend quickly to assess the damage Arthur might have endured.

Nothing could have had prepared Caleb for what the boy saw next.

"Oh God Arthur, you've got some deep wounds on your chest. We need to stop the bleeding before you bleed out." Caleb said frantically applying pressure on the wound to help prevent his friend from bleeding out.

"I don't have any bandages, but we can use the fire striker to cauterize the wound. It's going to hurt, but it's our only option." Arthur said between his labored breaths

"Okay man, I'll start the fire. Just hold on for me, Arthur." Caleb said as he quickly tried to search, and gather enough materials for a fire.

Arthur knew that he was now in dire strait as he struggled with the severity of his new injury.

He knew that he had to hold on with every fiber of his being, because the boy still needed him.

Then after a few minutes Caleb had gathered up some saved tinder bundles he had stored in his bag. He assembled them together, and after successfully igniting it, he was able to start a fire with Arthur's fire striker.

Once that was done, he got Arthur's knife and cleaned the blade off with fresh rain water from outside to sterilize it as best as he could. Then he took the knife and he inserted it into the open flame slowly making sure it had enough heat to close the wounds of his friend who was now clinging on to dear life. "Okay Arthur this is definitely going to hurt, but we have to do it."

Arthur looked at the boy with a great sense of nervousness, but knew it needed to be done. "I know. Just do it quickly." He said closing his eye's as he readied himself for what was to come next.

Caleb quickly placed the burning blade flat on the open wound and Arthur screamed in agonizing pain. The echoes of his own cries radiated through the cave this time. Instead of a bear struggling to live, the cave was met with a cry of a man that was now dancing with the fires of hell, but refusing to give up and hold on with the fibers of his unwavering spirit.

Caleb hearing Arthur's cries found he had no choice but to cover his friend's mouth with his hand tightly with his free palm. He didn't want to do this, but did with reluctance so the wolves that were still lurking couldn't hear the man's scream.

With the flaming steel meeting exposed flesh, Caleb kept on cauterizing the man's wounds, but the pain was too much for Arthur, and he soon lost consciousness, but not his fight to live.

Once the deed was done, and he knew his friend was safe, Caleb gently lifted the ember burning knife to see if the wounds were completely closed. The teen was relieved to see it was closed, but had multiple blisters on it from the burns.

"We'll get you to the cabin, Arthur, we'll get you there don't worry." Caleb whispered to his friend. As he looked on with a deep sense of overwhelming emotion hidden under his face. The teen was aware that Arthur might never be the same after this.

Caleb's hands were still trembling as he let go of the hot iron knife in his palm. He had never done anything like what he just did before, but Arthur's life had depended on it. The older man was still lying unconscious on the ground, his breathing was still shallow and labored. Caleb knew that he had done everything he could to save his friends life, but now it was a waiting game.

As he took a moment himself, Caleb looked around the cave they were in, finally taking in their surroundings. He knew they were still far from any form of civilization. But the teen realized if they didn't get help soon, they would both soon die out here. Caleb wondered if they would even make it back to Arthur's cabin, which to his unknown knowledge was lying in wait only a few miles away. The boy still was clinging to hope in the time being, not for him but for Arthur.

Sighing heavily, Caleb leaned against the wall of the cave and closed his eyes. He was tired, scared, and unsure of what to do next. He wondered if they would ever get out of this alive. Or would death find them in this desolate place, or would they somehow make it far enough to find some form of safety.

While he sat there, lost in thought, Caleb rested nearby listening to the gentle rain outside the cave. The boy couldn't help, but wonder if it was mother nature just doing what she did best or was it the tears of God himself weeping over the pair's predicament.

He was still by Arthur's side making sure the man was still breathing, and responsive. One thing was definitely certain to him though, and that's that it was starting to look like it was going to be a very tough night.

It was probably a few hours that had gone by when Arthur finally stirred and started to wake up. "How long was I out for?" Arthur asked groggy, and disoriented.

"Just a couple hours. You were out cold, but it was for the best I think." Caleb said in a somber tone that went unforgotten to the man's ears.

"Why is that?" Arthur questioned turning his head to the boy's direction.

"Because you would've kept screaming your ass off, and we can't let these fucking wolves know we're compromised." Caleb spoke truthfully.

"Very true. I don't think I would have been able to stay quiet when that hurt like a bitch." Arthur said sitting up with obvious pain.

"Hey, take it easy man you've been through a lot today." Caleb said, pleading with his friend.

"Caleb I'm okay, I promise. If I wasn't I would let you know." Arthur said in a strained manner.

After a brief awkward moment of silence Arthur spoke up once more. "Any signs of the wolves anymore?"

"No, they haven't come this direction anymore I think. I heard what sounded like them taking down an elk about an hour ago, so if they did, they'll be distracted with that for a while."

"Okay then, that's enough rest for me. We need to get out of here before the pack comes around here again." Arthur said confidently.

"Can you even walk?" Caleb questioned his friend with concern.

"I'll try, just help me up if you can." Arthur motioned for the boy to come up and extended his arm as a sign he was ready to go.

Caleb helped Arthur up gingerly, and they slowly made their way out to the entrance of the cave.

Once Arthur balanced himself, it was Caleb who gathered their bags and was once again by his partner's side.

Arthur was feeling steady, but quickly felt the effects of motion sickness taking over him as he had rushed into things faster than he should have. And in response he had no choice but to bend over and vomit onto the ground to get some sort of relief from the very pain he was feeling.

Caleb grew more worried, and decided to speak up. "We need to find a way to get you proper medical attention."

"We will, but first we need to get to the cabin. Trust me, it's our only way." Arthur spoke with a look that was almost on the verge of pleading with the boy.

"Remember, survival is not just about the physical skills, Caleb. It's about the strength of your spirit, and the resilience of your faith." Arthur said with a newfound sense of purpose filling him.

"Alright I'll help you, as much as I can, Arthur." Caleb said still with a hint of reluctance.

"I know you will, Caleb. You're a brave kid." Arthur said as he padded the boy on his shoulder giving him a knowing nod of acknowledgement.

Caleb put one of Arthur's arms around his shoulder, and they proceeded onto their journey to the cabin.

Arthur's face was pale, his breaths coming in shallow gasps. The pain etched across his features was a constant reminder of the race against time. Caleb could see the determination in Arthur's eyes, a silent plea for them to reach the cabin before it was too late.

The path ahead was treacherous, littered with fallen branches and hidden roots. Caleb's feet stumbled over obstacles, but he gritted his teeth and pressed on, his grip on Arthur's arm never wavering. The forest seemed to tighten around them, the trees closing in, creating a claustrophobic atmosphere that added to the mounting tension.

As they plodded forward, Caleb's mind raced with thoughts of the dangers that lurked in the shadows. Would the wolves find them, drawn by the scent of Arthur's blood soaked clothes? Could they stumble into the territory of another predator? His imagination conjured images of the packs glowing eyes, sharp fangs, and the guttural growls of the creatures lurking just beyond their line of sight.

Arthur's labored breathing grew louder, and Caleb's heart sank. He knew they had to reach the cabin soon, or Arthur's chances of survival would dwindle further with each agonizing step.

Every second felt like an eternity as they fought against the unforgiving terrain and the weight of their fears.

Finally, after what seemed like hours of walking, they spotted the cabin in the distance. It was just like Arthur had left it, a rustic old cabin made of the finest logs and surrounded by snowdrifts. They quickened their pace, hoping to make it to safety before the wolves discovered them.

When they approached the cabin, they could see that the door was slightly ajar. Arthur motioned for Caleb to stay back as he cautiously pushed the door open with his bowie knife. He peered inside, but the cabin was empty just like he had left it. Not a voice, not a sound, just Arthur's old acquaintance solitude.

Arthur quickly lit a fire into the fireplace and set about reinforcing the door with Caleb's help. Once the pair knew it was set in place and could hold, Arthur proceeded to take care of their next problem like getting a change of clothes, and getting food.

But Little did Arthur know the real struggle was about to rise within him.

Chapter Seven:

The Hidden Note And Struggles

*O*nce everything was taken care of, Arthur and Caleb settled into the cabin, their hearts were still racing from the fear of being hunted by the wolves, and barely making it to the Cabin alive.

Not to mention that the bear attack still had their adrenaline rushing. They had both kept going until they were safely inside their dense wooden fortress, but as Arthur had started a fire, and worked with Caleb to fortify the door by the end of it all. The pair had just enough energy to collapse onto the old sofa exhausted, but they finally felt safe away from the dangers that laid in wait outside.

They were at long last free to let the heaviness of the events of the past few months finally catch up to them.

Arthur's body still ached from the grueling bear attack, and he felt like he had been hit by a truck. He knew he couldn't keep going like this, but he didn't know how to stop.

The exhaustion was overwhelming, and he felt like he was drowning in a sea of despair.

Caleb sat beside him, his eyes still wide with fear and concern. "Are we going to be okay Arthur." he whispered.

Arthur didn't know how to answer the boy. He wanted to tell Caleb that everything would be fine like he had been, but he couldn't bring himself to lie. The truth was that they were still in a dangerous situation, and he didn't know if they would make it out alive, just like the teen was hoping they could.

He was holding onto hope all this time, but it still felt like the more he tried the more impossible their circumstances became.

What had originally been a struggle for his own survival turned into protecting this teenage boy. It was the reason he had been fighting all this time, but now things felt like a downwards force of impending doom. As they still sat there the middle-aged survivalist could see the more daunting everything was beginning to feel. Including the tasks ahead, as well as the dread of how they kept experiencing things that almost brought them to their death.

Arthur wouldn't have been able to live with himself if he would've let something happen to the young teen, so he had been pushing on for the time being.

Now it just seemed like he couldn't do that correctly. He didn't know how much further he could go.

As he saw that Caleb had drifted off to sleep on the couch in the living room, Arthur moved to where he could sit alone in the darkness of his own bedroom, staring blankly at the wall with a whiskey bottle in hand that he had retrieved from the kitchen. He felt lost and isolated, and he didn't know how to keep the boy safe from the uncertainty that awaited them outside.

So Arthur alone in his room with his whiskey in hand did the only thing he knew how to do. He prayed to the heaven's with a battered body, and a cracked spirit.

"God it's me again." Arthur said as he sat there with his head bowed.

"I don't know what else to do. I got the kid here, but I don't know what more I can do to help him. I'm not physically capable to help him anymore." Arthur said trying not to let his voice fall with emotion.

"I don't know if you're even listening to me. I've been praying for strength and guidance, but I feel like I'm getting nowhere."

Arthur took a swig of his whiskey before continuing his prayer. "I can't protect him. He's just a boy, and I'm tired. Lord I'm so freaking tired. I need your help, I can't even keep myself up anymore. I need a sign, something to show me that you're still with me."

Arthur paused for a moment, looking up at the ceiling. "Right now, I want to give up. But I know that's not what you want for me, or for Caleb. I need your strength, your guidance, your love. Please, Lord, help me. Show me that I'm not alone in this. I need to know I can get this kid out of here to somewhere safe."

Arthur took another drunken sip of his room temp liquor, and waited for a response again. When none came, he sat the bottle down and lowered his head back down, weeping softly.

Arthur could feel all the steps falling into place for him to surrender. He couldn't go on any further.

But then when all seemed at a loss, something caught his eye. A glint of light reflected off a small object on the floor. He reached over and picked it up, and his heart skipped a beat when he saw what it was.

It was a note from his late wife Zoey, hidden away in his closet by his old fishing tackle box.

He had forgotten all about it from when he had originally got to the cabin, but now it felt like a lifeline, a message from beyond her grave.

He unfolded the note and read the words she had written to him so very long ago as he had prepared for his first job interview. "I believe in you," she had wrote. "You are strong enough to face anything that comes your way. Remember that I am always with you, forever, and always honey."

Fresh tears began to stream down Arthur's face as he read the note over and over again. He felt like his wife was there with him, giving him the strength to keep on going.

He held his head up staring at the ceiling so he could look beyond into the heaven's looking up to where she was, and their son who were now with God. He could feel the comfort they were giving him.

"Thank you God, and thank you my love. I know you all are with me." Arthur said with a teary eyed smile.

After his prayer was finished, Arthur dragged himself into his bathroom, so he could start taking care of his wounds. He attended to the claw marks from the bear attack that Caleb had cauterized, as well as the old wounds on his leg and forehead from the first wolf attack. Arthur knew that he needed to take care of himself properly, or else his injuries could become infected and lead to more serious problems.

He started an I.V. on himself, carefully administering fluids to help his body heal. He cleaned and redressed his wounds, trying to avoid any further damage. As he examined himself in the mirror, he refused to give up on Caleb, who needed the man's help to get out of these frozen Alaskan tundras.

When Arthur finally sat on the edge of the bathtub, his head was heavy and his body was drained of all its energy. He had left the I.V. hanging, trying to rehydrate himself, but even as he waited there, it felt like it was a monumental task in his current state. But alas Arthur sat there patiently for what felt like an eternity, his head was just like his body a throbbing mess covered in dry blood, and his old sweat with grime.

He could feel his mind start to drift back to the countless nights he spent with Caleb in their makeshift shelters, desperately trying to stay warm as the frigid Alaskan air whipped around them. He couldn't remember a time other than the death of his own family where he had never felt more helpless or vulnerable in his life.

While Arthur was reflecting on the multitude of events the pair went through, he could feel his body finally beginning to recover. He could feel a small sense of pride in what both he, and Caleb had both accomplished.

But that pride was quickly overshadowed by a deep sense of fatigue. He knew that he had pushed himself to the brink of his physical and mental limits, and he wasn't sure if he had anything left in him to keep going. The thought of returning to civilization and all of its comforts was both enticing and overwhelming. He was well aware after everything he had gone through that he could never be the same person he once was.

As he sat there, lost in thought, he realized once more that their expedition was far from over. There were still challenges ahead, still obstacles to overcome. And of course the weight of the pack still being out there lurking to strike haunted his mind.

Just as the I.V. was done, and he had finished taking care of himself, he heard Caleb knocking on his bedroom door, telling him about an issue with the floorboard. Arthur carefully made his way to the other room, where Caleb was waiting for him.

Caleb explained that when he had woken up needing to use the spare bathroom he had almost tripped over a loose floorboard and that he thought there might be something hidden underneath it.

While Arthur followed the boy into the living room, he as well noticed the loose floorboard that Caleb almost tripped over. Arthur gradually went to inspect it, and to their surprise, they found a hidden duffel emergency bag that Arthur had forgotten about. The bag was filled with Canned Ravioli, MRE packets, a hunting knife, four handguns, ammo, fresh clothes, and other survival gear. On top of the bag was a picture of Arthur's late wife Zoey and their late son Nicholas.

Caleb could see the grief in Arthur's eyes as he stared at the picture. Arthur couldn't hold it in, and broke down crying, catching his friend by surprise. But if the boy would have asked Arthur what was wrong. The man in that moment would've told him, it was because of the note he had found only moments ago.

But Arthur still being the boy's friend managed to tell Caleb how much he missed them and how he wished they were still here with him. Caleb tried to console him, but he could see that Arthur was still deeply affected by the memory of his wife and son.

After a few more minutes, Arthur composed himself and showed Caleb some of the items in the bag. He explained how each item was important for their continued survival, and he even demonstrated how to use the hunting knife and handguns he had in the bag.

Caleb of course knew most of the information, but listened intently as this time it was Arthur's turn to share his knowledge with him, and he began to appreciate the importance of how Arthur was prepared for anything. He realized that Arthur's passion for survivalism was not just about being paranoid or fearful, but it was about being responsible and ready to face any hurdles that life may throw their way.

After they left the room, Caleb felt grateful for the experience and for the opportunity to learn from Arthur. He knew that he had a lot left to learn from his friend, but was feeling humbled to have a teacher with as much experience as his mentor had.

It was the very next day in the morning when Arthur started off by explaining the importance of setting up a trip wire as an early warning system to detect any approaching wolves that might venture off into their area. It was important to him that they stayed alert at all cost. They couldn't afford anymore close calls, and he needed to show the boy that getting ahead of the pack was their first step on getting out of these woods.

As they went outside Arthur showed Caleb how to tie a strong piece of paracord between two trees at a low height and how to attach an old beer can or other noise-making objects to the cord. Arthur also gave Caleb some tips on how to camouflage their trip wire so that it would not be easily visible to any potential threats other than the wolves.

Next, Arthur demonstrated how to set up traps around the cabin to catch any other animals that might try to break in. He showed Caleb how to use a different type of snare trap and how to place it in the right location to effectively capture the target animal. Arthur in addition showed Caleb how to make a few other types of traps using materials they found in the woods that the kid didn't even know about himself.

Caleb was mesmerized by the skill set of Arthur. He could finally see what the older hunter was truly made of now that he was in his element.

Despite still healing from his injuries, Arthur was patient and thorough in his instructions, making sure Caleb understood each step before moving on to the next. The boy was eager to learn more and worked hard to put Arthur's lessons into practice.

Arthur's injuries did however slow him down a bit, but he was grateful for the chance to teach Caleb these skills. He knew that with these tools, Caleb would be better equipped to handle the challenges they kept having to face as a team.

It was by the end of the day, Arthur and Caleb succeeded in setting up their trip wires and traps, and their cabin was well-protected from any potential threats. Caleb was thankful for Arthur's guidance, and Arthur was proud of the skills he had passed on to his young friend.

But as they were preparing dinner that night over the old gas stove in the Cabin, Caleb noticed that Arthur couldn't stop coughing.

Caleb asked his friend if he was okay in which Arthur replied with a quick scoff, and smile. Brushing passed the subject to derail the boy's thoughts of worry Arthur changed the conversation.

"So Caleb, you never told me where you and your dad were originally from." Arthur tried his best to lightened the mood.

"Well I was born in Portland, but my father was a doctor from Galilee. My mother she was from Alaska, but died giving birth to me. My parents they were a part of this medical travel group of doctors. They'd go to each state, and assist the poor. At least that's what my dad would tell me."

Arthur nodded slowly understanding more of the boy's past. "So what made you and your dad travel back up to Alaska."

"My mom had my grandpa here so my dad wanted to look after him as it was one of my mother's last wishes." Caleb replied with a warm smile that showed his fondness over the memories of his family.

Arthur returned the boy's smile as he stood by the stove.

"So is it okay if I ask you a question since we're on the subject man." Caleb said looking at his mentor with a hopeful stare.

"Sure that seems fair enough kid. Go for it I'm an open book." Arthur said with a light chuckle.

"Your son Nicholas what was he like?" Caleb asked with curiosity in his voice.

Arthur's stirring of the canned ravioli he had been preparing for them stopped, along with his smile which slowly turned into a serious expression.

"He was a lot like you." Arthur said in a somber voice before continuing.

"He was silly, bright, and full of life just like you, kid. He never let anyone be sad or angry." Arthur smiled lightly remembering his boy.

"I remember every morning before I left for work, he and I would eat breakfast together while Zoey slept in. She worked nights at Norton Sound Regional hospital. You know the one on Greg Avenue." Arthur pointed in a random direction to emphasize his point.

"Yeah, yeah my dad went there for business sometimes!" Caleb said with enthusiasm.

"Yeah so me and Nicholas would have our bonding time in the mornings. That's what I miss most." Arthur stood there in silence for a moment as he reflected on the cherished memories he once shared with his son.

"I'm so sorry Arthur." Caleb said looking at his friend with a sad expression that showed he shared the pain with his friend.

"Hey kid it's alright, to be honest you remind me a lot like him. I think you two would've been great friends." Arthur said with a weakened smile.

"And I'm sure you would've been friends with my dad if he was still here." Caleb said with his own smile in return.

"Thanks kid. What do you say about having enough with this sad sob moment, and start getting cleaned up for dinner huh!" Arthur hollered positively, while clapping his hands together which made Caleb laugh.

As Caleb was in the bathroom, Arthur was still in the kitchen almost through with cooking dinner for him, and the boy. The aroma was filling his nostrils when he suddenly felt a wave of nausea wash over him.

Arthur had to take a step back from the stove trying to get ahold of himself, but it was no use. He stumbled over to his bedroom and ended up collapsing on the wooden floor, as he was feeling weak and dizzy. Caleb who was just opening the bathroom door took notice of this, and rushed over to his friends side, concerned.

"Are you okay, Arthur?" Caleb asked, his young teenage face filled with worry.

Arthur shook his head weakly. "I don't know, kid. I feel terrible." The man tried sitting up, but had to hold onto Caleb's shoulder for aid.

Caleb quickly took measure and helped Arthur into bed and covered him with blankets.

"What can I do to help." Caleb asked trying to assist Arthur more.

"Get my medical bag under the sink in the bathroom." Arthur said between his returning labored breaths.

As Caleb rushed into the bathroom to retrieve the orange colored duffel bag. Arthur still struggled in bed as he vomited into his trashcan that was by his bedside.

When Arthur was done blowing chunks as he liked to call it, he saw Caleb looking inside the medical bag to see the I.V. bags of fluids, and medical supplies that he had inside.

The Seasoned survivalist then called the teen back into the room to proceed in getting him stabilized. The room was still spinning, and he knew he needed to take care of this so he didn't pass out.

When The teen had returned to the room he became aware that Arthur had grown pale, and was now sweating excessively.

In return Caleb's helplessness only grew as he saw his mentor, and friend suffering more than he already had. "What else do you need me to do." He asked Arthur getting a feeling what the man might have in mind already.

"I'm going to need you to give me an I.V. I'll show you how to do it, but we need to act quickly. I think I'm just dehydrated." Arthur said weakly.

Caleb couldn't help his reaction as he stood frozen there nervously by Arthur's bedside, holding the medical bag he had just retrieved. He knew he hadn't done anything like this before, but Caleb knew that Arthur needed these I.V. fluids hung right away and he didn't want to wait for his friend to fall sicker than he already was.

But still he didn't know why he had become so nervous. He'd helped the same exact man in the woods, and even cauterized his wounds from a bear attack, so why was this simple task bothering him so much.

Arthur looked up at Caleb, and could see the teen was scared. In that moment Arthur remembered he was just a kid lost in the woods still. A boy who'd lost his father, and was running away from any kind of danger all this time.

So with a weakened, but yet reassuring smile Arthur spoke up. "Don't worry kid. It's not as hard as it looks and I'll be right here to help the whole time," he spoke lightly before gesturing to the I.V. bag and tubing that the teen held onto.

Caleb took a deep breath and nodded, once again trying to steady his nerves. He understood he'd never even seen his dad or anyone else for that matter administer an I.V. or I.V. fluids before, but he was aware that he had to try in order to help Arthur.

First The man walked Caleb through the steps, explaining how to properly clean the site and insert the needle into the vein in the right spot. Caleb listened closely, trying to remember every detail.

While he began to insert the sharp pointer, Caleb's hands shook slightly, but Arthur proceeded to gently guide him through the process. "You're doing great, Caleb," he said sincerely. "Just take it slow and steady."

Caleb could see the needle enter the vain of Arthur's arm sliding into place smoothly. He held pressure, and retrieved a I.V. bandage with tape to secure it.

Finally after what seemed like hours, but was only a mere few minutes, the I.V. was in place and it was taped down. Arthur then showed Caleb how to hang the bag of fluids above the bed. "There you go. You did it kid," he said, patting Caleb on the back.

Caleb felt a surge of pride and relief wash over him. He had been so nervous, but with his friends guidance, he had successfully administered the I.V. the right way. He knew he still had more to learn to help Arthur, but this experience had given the young teenager a newfound confidence in his ability to keep helping the only friend he had.

"Thanks again kid," Arthur said, smiling weakly. "I don't know what I would have done if you weren't here."

"You'd probably be dead dude." Caleb said with a laugh.

"Yeah you're probably right. I definitely would've been if you hadn't found me that day we met." Arthur chuckled lightly before drifting off to sleep.

As soon as Arthur was semi stable, and sleeping Caleb went to finish cooking dinner, knowing that they both needed to eat to keep their strength up.

But as Arthur lay in bed trying to sleep, he began to feel worse despite the I.V. fluids. He noticed he came down with a fever that was rapidly spiking, and he started to have hallucinations. He saw visions of his late wife, Zoey, and his late son, Nicholas. They were both smiling at him in the corner of the room, as if to reassure him that everything would be okay.

"You guy's aren't supposed to be here. You aren't real." Arthur said trying to shake it out of his head.

"Honey it's okay just rest. We're here for you." Zoey's soft voice echoed through the walls of the room.

"No this can't be happening, you aren't real! You aren't here, get out please." Arthur pleaded with the visions trying his best to snap out of it.

"Honey you need to rest, just relax." The voice of Zoey rang through his ears, and before he could truly process it Arthur felt her soft hand stroke the side of his face.

Arthur slowly started to relax as each flash of the memories of his family flooded him. He knew they were gone, but in the moment he just paused to enjoy that single touch that he had missed.

Despite the comfort of these visions, Arthur still couldn't shake the feeling of dread that had started to creep into the pit of his stomach. He was still aware that he was in the middle of nowhere, with no access to proper medical care. So it was with that Arthur came to realize that if he didn't get better soon, he might not be able to get passed whatever was happening to him.

Before the survivalist could start to think about the situation further, Arthur found himself once again becoming dizzy, but this time it was starting to overtake him, and before he could call out to Caleb for help, everything went dark.

When Caleb walked back into Arthur's room with a plate of food, he was thrown off guard to see his mentor having a grand mal seizure in the bed. The man was thrashing wildly, and was beginning to foam at the mouth.

In a desperate attempt Caleb dropped the plate, and rushed to the bed where he turned the man onto his side to prevent choking. He had remembered this tip from when he was younger. His grandfather had epilepsy, and his father would do this every time the elder would have a seizure.

Caleb held onto his friends body as Arthur was riding the convulsions for several minutes.

When Arthur finally stopped seizing, and stopped convulsing Caleb laid him on his back to rest.

Once Caleb knew the seizure wasn't coming back, the teen took this opportunity to check on the man's chest wounds, and noticed how discolored the claw marks were. Caleb quickly realized that something was seriously wrong, and his friend was beginning to show signs of sepsis or a severe form of staph infection.

Caleb knew that sepsis was a life-threatening condition caused by some type of infection typically staph, and he knew that he had to act fast to save Arthur's life. The teen then remembered reading about the slippery elm plant, which was known for its medicinal properties. He had remembered reading about it in his dad's office a few years prior, so he was fully aware that the herbal remedy could help to probably treat a heavy infection like the one Arthur was suffering through.

Caleb believed that the plant grew in the Alaskan woods, so he knew there was a strong chance to save Arthur, but in return he might need to set off on foot to find it by himself.

As Caleb sat there by his friends bedside where Arthur still laid in bed recovering from his seizure. He chose to try to talk to his unconscious mentor about this terrifying choice. "How are you feeling man." He asked with the best calming voice he could muster in that moment.

But the only reply that came back was silence like the cold harsh winds outside. Letting the boy know that Arthur was not going to wake up anytime soon.

Caleb feeling more helpless cried softly sitting there, struggling with his decision, but he knew he had no choice on what he needed to do. If Arthur didn't get help fast his infection would certainly get worse, and he could die.

"Arthur I don't know if you can hear me man, but I need to go back into the woods and find something I think might help you feel better. I know you wouldn't want me going alone, but I need to try."

He waited another moment for a reply, but the middle-aged man was still unresponsive.

Caleb spoke again to try and get his friend to respond to any of his statements as a last go-ahead. "I remember a book in my dad's office, and how it talked about how the natives used this plant to treat infections In the blood, and other illnesses as well. I'm going to try to find it and bring it back to you." Caleb leaned over and patted Arthur's arm.

"Just hang in there, I'll be back soon." As soon as Caleb cleaned up the spilled food in the room he went to the living room area towards the duffel bag, and got Arthur's bowie knife, as well as a handgun just in case. He then bundled up before heading outside in the cold blistering wind, and into the woods.

"Here we go." Caleb said to himself as he was greeted by the familiar cold harsh Alaskan winds.

While the teen trudged through the fresh snowy underbrush his mind was racing with worry; he could feel a sense of panic rising. He had never been in such a dire circumstance like this before, but he didn't know how else to help Arthur.

Finally, after what seemed like hours of searching, and searching Caleb collapsed in a clearing, tears of frustration streaming down his face. He felt lost and helpless, unable to find the plant that Arthur needed to survive.

But as he sat there, along with his mind racing with fear and doubt, he remembered something that Arthur had been teaching him all this time: "Survival is not just about the physical skills, Caleb. It's about the strength of your spirit, and the resilience of your faith."

With those thoughts ringing in his ears, Caleb took a deep breath and stood up. He knew that he couldn't give up now, no matter how hopeless the situation seemed. He would keep searching, keep looking for the slippery elm plant, and do everything in his power to help his friend live.

And with that determination in his heart, Caleb set off even deeper into the woods once more, his eyes scanning the trees and the ground for any sign of the elusive plant. He knew that this had already been a difficult journey, but he also had realized that he had to keep going for Arthur, and for himself.

After he searched for a while more, he finally found the plant he had been looking for hidden behind a bush. He carefully picked copious amounts of it just in case.

His hands were shivering from the cold as he put the plant in his backpack. The sharp edges of the Alaskan winds were cutting into the boy's face like razor blades.

When Caleb was finally finished, and had the herb packed, and feeling comfortable with his mission, a sudden thought occurred to the teen. What if he could also search for more of the fire weeds for tea to help Arthur.

He was aware that the winds were picking up, and he had already got what he had needed. But Arthur needed as much help for his immune system as he could get to up his chances of survival.

It was with that strenuous thought Caleb chose to make his way deeper into the forest.

Caleb looked as far as his body would take him, but to no avail in finding what he needed for the tea.

His body was now aching, and his mind was starting to cloud. These were symptoms he was all too familiar with as he had faced hypothermia before. The boy knew he was pushing his own limits beyond even what he had faced prior.

Caleb didn't want to give up though, he was as determined as the unrelenting cold surrounding him. But one thing was for certain, and that's that time was of the essence.

It was only after a short time while he was looking a bit deeper that Caleb noticed that he was being followed. The young survivor could hear the distant sound of quite Paws, and twigs breaking. And there was no mistaking it. He knew it was the pack stalking him from afar.

As he turned he could see in the distance the pack were already closing in on him fast. Caleb knew that he had to defend himself, so he pulled out his hand gun quickly and began to shoot at the wolves with swift shots.

Caleb was still a young skilled marksman in his own right, but the wolves were always relentless. He was forced to keep running, shooting at the wolves as he ran as fast as possible without error.

The chase was intense, and Caleb was beginning to tire. Just when he thought he couldn't run any further, he saw one of the trip wires Arthur and him had set up previously.

He quickly jumped over it, and when the wolves snagged it, it caused a tree branch to fling its way into multiple of the unforgiving animals causing them to drop dead in the snow.

The rest of the wolves that were behind them fled in terror which gave Caleb a chance to calm down from the adrenaline rush that had been coursing through his body.

As he looked at the three animals dead on the ground, Caleb could feel the realization of how close he had come to being killed. The boy knew that this situation was still as serious as it had ever been, but he was now even more aware that it was still necessary to stay vigilant at all cost.

After a brief moment to catch his breath, Caleb was soon able to make his way back to the cabin.

When Caleb entered the fortress of solitude he went straight to the room with the plant in hand. Where he then started to mash it into a fine paste for Arthur's infected wounds. Once the paste was applied to his friends damaged chest, Caleb went into the kitchen to see if there was something in the pantry he could hopefully use for tea.

When he stumbled upon a bottle of turmeric he thought he had struck gold. Caleb knew that the bright orange colored spice was a super charge herb for the immune system.

Just when the teen was done making the tea, and made his way over back to the bedroom, he was met with disappointment as he noticed that Arthur was still unconscious. "Come on Arthur, wake up." But again no reply ever came.

The teen waited.. for his friends voice, a sound, a sign, just something. But all that greeted his adolescent ears was Arthur's former companion solitude.

So Caleb sat there anxiously by Arthur's bedside, watching as his mentor lay motionless, his breathing still shallow and lacking. He had prayed over the herb that he had applied to treat Arthur's infection, but it had been several minutes and there was still no sign of any improvement.

As time ticked by, Caleb's worry turned into panic. He called out Arthur's name, again and again hoping for some response, but there was still none. He shook him gently, hoping to rouse him from his slumber, but still nothing.

Finally, Caleb's frustration and fear boiled over, and he let out a primal scream, smashing a nearby vase in his rage. He cried out for his friend to wake up, to come back to him, but still Arthur laid there motionless.

The teen hit the wall beside his friends bedside repeatedly as he screamed his lungs out. "WAKE UP, WAKE UP DAMMIT." the boy cried out with desperation, but to no avail.

Caleb sank to the floor, tears streaming down his face as he realized the gravity of the situation. Arthur had been his mentor, and only friend up to this point. Guiding him through some of the toughest times of his young life. He couldn't bear the thought of losing another person that meant so much to him. Not again.

While sitting there on the hardwood floor crying his soul out for only God to hear his anguish. Caleb still sat there longer, but he was growing more impatient by each passing moment in time.

He still prayed, but his hope was dwindling down as the more time passed. He was in the room eating one of Arthur's protein bars after a few more hours had passed of him lying in wait. When the time finally arrived, Caleb noticed Arthur start to begin to stir Back to life. "Caleb...is that you. What happened?" Arthur said weakly.

"Yeah, it's me. You had a grand mal seizure, I had to stabilize you. After that I used a herb I found in the woods called the slippery elm plant to make a paste, because your wounds became infected. You were showing the signs of sepsis I think that's what they call it. It's a type of infection in the blood. So, I did what I had to do." Caleb said as he handed Arthur the tea he had prepared.

Arthur smiled weakly feeling grateful for the boy's assistance in trying to get him better. But more importantly he was forever blessed to have had a friend go so far to save his life.

"Thank you, Caleb. You're a good kid." Arthur said as the man took a careful sip of his tea before he paused for a moment. "So, you went out into the woods by yourself?" He asked with raised eyebrows of curiosity.

Caleb nodded slowly as he confirmed Arthur's word's. "Yeah, I did. I needed to help you, Arthur you were dying."

Arthur looked again impressed by the stones Caleb had, to make such a risk wasn't just gutsy, but it took skill. "You sure do got a set on you boy, but you make a damn good partner."

Caleb couldn't help, but laugh in return. "Yeah, well we're a team, right man."

Arthur nodded before giving the boy a fist bump of trust. In which Caleb returned gladly.

The pair came to find out something that night, and that was that, no matter how bad it got nothing could break this bond they had formed together.

Finally, after a week of struggling, Arthur's fever broke. He was weak but still alive. He would look over at Caleb, who was sleeping on a nearby cot, and would feel an overwhelming amount of gratitude for the boy who had saved his life once again.

While he lay there, trying to continue his recovery, Arthur thought about his visions of Zoey and Nicholas. He knew that they were gone, but he couldn't help but feel comforted by the thought that they were watching over him. He recounted once again that he had to keep going, for their sake, but also now for the boy that kept saving his life.

Meanwhile the night had worn on, and Arthur got up from his bed carefully, slowly walking with diligence to the window where he put his head to the glass, listening intently. The howls outside they were faint, but he knew they were there.

He could sense their hunger, their desperation for prey. He knew that they were still very much a threat to him and Caleb.

The man wasn't stupid, he knew that they were waiting for him and the boy to just make that one mistake. That was all the pack needed, but Arthur wasn't going to let them win this fight.

Arthur turned slowly, looking at Caleb and felt a renewed surge of protectiveness. He was aware that the boy was his responsibility, and he was determined to get him to safety. He had been preparing for this moment all this time. He knew that it was now a race against the clock, and that every minute counted.

Arthur paced back and forth slowly, his mind racing with the thoughts of survival. He understood that he had to be careful, that one wrong move could mean the difference between life and death. But he was determined to get Caleb to Civilization, even if it meant sacrificing himself in the process.

Arthur looked out the window once more, his eyes scanning the darkness for any signs of movement. He could feel the tension building inside him, the adrenaline now pumping through his veins. He knew that the wolves were getting closer, and they were thirsty for his blood. What they didn't know was that Arthur was now thirsty for their blood as well.

It was at this moment Arthur lowered his head in thought and spoke to himself softly. "Caleb and I won't be just another notch on their belt. We'll be the one's they never forget, the one's who get away."

Chapter Eight:

The Weight of Purpose

It was only after a week of healing that Arthur found himself once again stirring the contents of a meal for himself, and Caleb. Only this time it was one of the MRE packets from the duffel bag, the aroma of the hot insulated meal filled the rustic cabin.

Caleb sat across from Arthur, where he was watching with hunger in his eyes. It had been a few weeks since they had each eaten a decent meal without something occurring, and the MRE was a welcome change from the canned ravioli, and hunted wild grouse they had been consuming up to this point.

After everything the pair had just gone through, this was the first sense of calmness either one of them had in a long time. It was peaceful, but also a somber moment in a way.

They found it was a time to grieve from the past, nurse their wounds, and process who'd they become. They realized they were now forever changed, and the heaviness of that weight was something that they both had to embrace with open arm's.

The loss and pain they each had been through was more then one person had to ever endure in a single lifetime. But they were both survivors who hadn't given up on their journey, and kept going while pushing each other to stay determined in the midst of already overwhelming odds.

Both survivors knew they had been through a multitude of events that had tested their survival skills to their limit thus far. The multiple encounters with the pack and even the bear, not to mention the unforgiving weather that had tried to force them to succumb to the elements of mother nature. It was all an overwhelming shit-storm that just kept rising with the tides.

But they refused to give up, and knew they had each other to lean on, because they weren't just friends, they were now family.

Caleb and Arthur couldn't help, but feel a deep sense of appreciation for the gift of life. They believed that surviving in the Alaskan woods was a heavy task, but they also understood that the gift of life was nothing to ever take for granted.

So while they sat at the dining room table, Arthur and Caleb felt a strange sense of peace and contentment. They were grateful for the lessons they had both learned and the experiences they had both shared, and they understood that they would always cherish the memories of their friendship in the Alaskan wilderness despite the dangers they had to face.

Arthur who was considering himself lucky to be alive, even given his multiple brushes with death was still moving slowly, but he was aware he was out of the woods for the time being in his recovery.

He was forever grateful to Caleb who had saved his ass on multiple occasions at this point, and Arthur knew that was something that could never be forgotten.

Caleb on the other hand was just happy to finally have a friend, and mentor. All those years running from everything, and anything it was a hellish nightmare he thought he'd have to face alone forever.

But when he met Arthur, he recognized that his life would never be the same again. He had come to see the older hunter as a father figure, and someone he could count on to be there no matter what challenges came at them.

Together as they ate, the pair started to discuss their options for finding a way to civilization. Caleb had suggested they follow the river path, which he believed would lead them to Girdwood if his hunch was correct.

Arthur was a bit hesitant, knowing that they were still in dangerous wolf territory. The pack was still out there, watching and waiting for their opportunity to strike.

Not to mention he was questioning if he was even well enough for the harsh environment that was awaiting them outside. But the survivalist was aware he still had to try.

A journey to Girdwood would be a fleeting task for him, and the kid which lead to a question the grizzled hunter couldn't help, but ask himself. Was he ready for it or was he about to embark on a suicide mission that would get him, and Caleb killed.

Arthur's thoughts drifted as the pair ate in a calm but cold silence, the weight of purpose was once more, heavy on his mind.

He had believed that he was meant to do something important in his life, something that would make a difference in the world ever since losing his family. Now, he believed that his purpose was to protect Caleb, to ensure that the kid made it back to civilization safely.

Arthur acknowledged that he might not be able to change the world, but he could change the view of how Caleb saw it.

He knew the boy had seen his fair share of shit, but he needed to show Caleb there was more to life than this.

Even though the boy had saved his life numerous times, he also gave Arthur something he hadn't had in a long time, and that was friendship.

But as he sat there, he still understood that the pack was still a threat, and that they needed to be attentive if they were going to survive. Arthur was also fully aware that if it came down to it he might need to be a casualty in order to keep Caleb safe. He couldn't bear the thought of something happening to the teen, not after everything they had been through together.

Arthur looked up from his meal and watched Caleb as the boy ate, a pang of guilt washing over him. He hadn't told the kid about his fears, about the weight of his purpose. He didn't want to scare him, didn't want him to think that they were doomed. Not after everything they had suffered through as a team.

But he also acknowledged that Caleb was a smart individual, and that he deserved to know the truth. Even if it meant letting the teen know what might happen when they ventured back out into the unforgiving wilderness.

"Hey, Caleb," Arthur said, his voice quiet. "There's something I need to tell you." The middle-aged survivalist said calmly running his hand through his now thickened beard.

Caleb looked up from his already half eaten meal, his eyes meeting Arthur's.

"What is it?" he asked, his voice was calm as the chill wind outside the cabin.

Arthur took a deep breath, trying to find the right words. He could feel his heart in his throat as his emotions started to show.

"I…I think my purpose has been to protect you even if I don't make it out there," he said finally. "To make sure that you make it back to civilization safe."

Caleb's expression softened, and the boy reached across the table to place a hand on Arthur's shoulder.

"You don't have to do that alone man," he said. "We'll protect each other just like we've been doing."

Arthur smiled, grateful for the boy's kindness and understanding. He knew that he could trust Caleb, but his mind still struggled with the thoughts of the unknown running over him.

The two Survivors still ate their meal in calm silence, but each of them were lost in their own thoughts. Not exactly sure what lay ahead for them.

As Caleb sat there at the table he couldn't believe what he had just heard his best friend say. He had grown to respect and admire Arthur over the course of their journey. He couldn't bear the thought of losing the only friend he had. Not when he already went over and beyond to make sure Arthur stayed alive.

Caleb could feel a lump start to form in his throat as he ate quietly struggling with his own thoughts. He didn't want to leave Arthur behind. And he was going to make sure he did everything in his power so it wouldn't need to come down to that.

They were a team, a unit, best friends, and most of all they were a family.

Soon after they were done eating, Arthur and Caleb had started to once again discuss their plan to leave the cabin and find their way to civilization. They went over the duffel bag they had found one more time to make sure they had everything they needed.

They saw that they still had two bowie knives and four handguns with ammo, not to mention Arthur's rifle and Caleb's crossbow. They had enough supplies to last them for a few more days, but they knew they needed to be careful.

They needed to ration their supplies if they were going to make it to Girdwood. They understood that it would be tough, but they could do it with enough determination.

While they went through the bag, Arthur looked too the corner of the room, and noticed that Caleb was running low on crossbow bolts. He knew they needed to replenish their supply, so he helped Caleb build more ammo by carving more arrows for him later that same day.

Together as they worked, Arthur could feel that his mind still wandered. The Survivalist was struggling to listen to his own gut telling him that this was most likely the calm right before the storm for what was going to be the biggest fight of their lives.

Behind him Caleb sat on the sofa cleaning his handguns thinking about what awaited them out there in the wilderness. He could feel his primal instinct start to come to the surface again, letting him know that it was getting closer for their journey.

You could hear a pen drop as Arthur and Caleb silently packed their backpacks and loaded their weapons, preparing themselves for this unknown war against the pack.

The two Survivors were fully aware that this might not end well, but they were determined to be ready, to fight with everything they had, and finally take down the monsters that had wanted to kill them all this time.

As they gathered their supplies and weapons, Arthur and Caleb started to talk about the wave of possibilities they might face. The team knew from everything that they had went through, that the wolves were fast, vicious, and that all it took was a single bite that could cause the situation to turn fatal. But they also had acknowledged that they had to keep standing their ground and fight back if they wanted to find civilization – there was no turning back now. This was going to be their final journey.

Arthur and Caleb both were still conquerors up until now, but they recognized that this final battle was going to be the moment of truth they had been building up to all this time.

They were calm and collected, but their words still became few as they were focused on the danger that was awaiting them in the distance. But they still understood that they weren't alone in this. They still had each other and they were in this struggle together no matter what.

Arthur grabbed his bowie knife and looked over at Caleb, determination written on both of their faces. They nodded at each other, agreeing that they would fight together until the end. They were warriors and they would either rise as a team or they would die as a team. But yet Arthur still couldn't shake off the feeling of uncertainty that hung over his own fate.

As he looked up and down the cabin one final time and prepared to leave with Caleb on their unknown voyage, Arthur decided to go into his bedroom for a lone moment of prayer.

He knew for certain that it was needed before venturing off outside with the boy into parts unknown to him.

Arthur could feel the hand of God over him, but the middle-aged survivalist needed more. He wanted to hear God's voice of reassurance to let him know that it would be okay.

It was after a while in the room, Arthur was still kneeling at the side of his bed with his hands clasped together, his eyes closed, and his head bowed. He had been praying for the past half-hour, asking God for the strength and protection he needed for the final journey he was about to embark on with Caleb.

"Dear God," Arthur had originally began, his voice shaky. "I know that the journey I'm about to go on is dangerous, and I don't know what the future holds. But I ask you to be with me every step of the way. Protect me, and Caleb from harm and give us the strength we need to face any challenges that come our way."

Arthur's thoughts then turned more to his friend Caleb, who he knew was just as terrified as he was. Arthur was aware that the teenage boy was still that just a boy, and he didn't want any more harm to come to the kid. Yes Caleb had helped Arthur survive, but Arthur knew he was still a lost boy.

"I ask you to watch over the kid please, Lord," Arthur continued. "He's just a boy, and he has been through enough, and I don't want him facing anymore then what he already has. Please help me to keep him safe from the dangers out there and guide us both to safety."

Arthur's thoughts then turned to the wolves that he knew would be a threat to them on their expedition. He knew that they had to be prepared for the worst, and he was willing to do whatever it takes to protect Caleb.

"If it comes to it, Lord, I'm ready to sacrifice myself for Caleb's safety," Arthur said with conviction. "But I ask that you give me the strength to protect him without it needing to come down to that if it's possible."

As Arthur opened his eyes, he noticed something underneath the bed frame by his knee. It was an old metal tin box that he had forgotten about. Inside he found a Grenade he remembered obtaining during an evening he had bonding with his father in-law a few years prior, and he had stashed it away on each survival trip he made for emergencies. He couldn't help, but chuckle thinking he could've used the damn thing in the beginning of all this.

"Wow I must be one stupid son of a bitch, if I forgot about this girl. You sure are gorgeous, but darling I know how deadly you can be." Arthur said laughing as he held the tiny explosive.

Arthur hesitated for a minute, unsure if he should bring the grenade on their journey. But after several moments of deliberation, he decided to pack it away in his backpack, just in case.

"I really hope I never have to use this," Arthur said to himself, zipping up his backpack. "But it's better to be more prepared then the first time."

With that final statement, Arthur stood up and made his way to the door, ready to face whatever awaited him, and Caleb

After an hour of waiting Caleb went to knock on Arthur's bedroom, but before his knuckles could come into contact with the wooden door, it opened.

"Are you okay man?" Caleb asked with concern as the bedroom door opened swiftly.

Arthur said nothing, but nodded with a smile that now had hidden meaning. He put his backpack over his shoulder, and helped Caleb put his on.

"Are you ready kid." Arthur asked with determination, and a strange tone of reassurance.

Caleb stood there nervous for a moment shaking in his boots. His hands gripping the straps of his backpack so tight, that his nails almost broke the skin of his palm's.

Arthur quickly noticing this, walked up to the boy where he put his hands on his shoulders for comfort. "It's going to be okay son".

Caleb nodded before giving the man as big of a hug as he could. The teen took this moment to slip something into the man's back-pocket of his backpack silently.

It went unnoticed too Arthur as he was busy trying to comfort the boy's nerves.

After Caleb quickly wiped his tears away, Arthur asked if he was okay. Even though the boy couldn't speak, because he was worried his voice might crack he extended his hand in a fist bump where Arthur gladly accepted.

Following this moment of reassurance, Arthur stood in the entryway, his weathered hands clutching the doorknob tightly. He glanced over at Caleb who now stood beside him, and it was in that moment Arthur knew that he owed the boy more than he could ever repay.

"Before we go, I have something for you," Arthur said, his voice gruff.

He reached into his front pocket of his backpack and pulled out a small, crumpled Twinkie, the last one that he had saved for his last meal originally that first night before everything happened. He handed it to the teen, who looked at him surprised.

"I know it's not much, but it was supposed to go with my last meal before i... well you know," Arthur said, his eyes misting over. "And I want you to have it. You deserve it."

The boy gladly took the Twinkie, a small smile tugging at the corners of his mouth. "Thanks, Arthur," he said softly.

Arthur nodded, his gaze fixed on the only true friend he had since losing his family. "But more than that, I want to thank you for saving me," he said, his voice barely above a whisper. "You saved me from myself, from giving up."

The boy looked at him, his expression now becoming serious. "You don't owe me anything, Arthur," he said. "I was just doing what anyone else would do."

Arthur shook his head slightly with his emotions obvious. "No, you don't understand. I was lost, both physically and mentally. I had given up hope. But you never gave up on me. You kept pushing me, encouraging me, and because of you, I made it out of those situations alive. And I'm a better man for it."

Caleb nodded slowly, his eyes shining with understanding. "I'm glad I could help, Arthur," he said, his voice soft right on the verge of breaking.

Arthur smiled, a genuine, heartfelt smile. Before adding "Me too, kid. Me too."

Together they exited out the entrance, of the cabin, where they knew it was time to go on a journey to war.

When Arthur and Caleb started to once again venture on through the cold harsh woods, they could see their breaths visible in the frigid air. The winds were relentless, but not impossible. They stayed on high alert for the pack of wolves that had been hunting them, because they knew these animals were still lurking in the distance, so they kept a watchful eye out as they started following the bed of water, Caleb had mentioned during their planning.

The wind was now becoming brutal, howling and biting at their skin, but they pushed on. They knew that they had to keep moving if they wanted to survive. As they walked, the snow changed to fog which began to thicken around them, making it hard to see more than a few feet in front of them.

Caleb shivered, pulling his black coat tighter around him. "This fog is getting really bad," he said, his voice barely audible over the sound of the unforgiving wind.

Arthur nodded in agreement, his eyes scanning the surrounding trees. "We need to keep moving," he said. "We can't stay out in the open like this."

They continued on, their footsteps silently crunching in the snow. But still the sound seemed to echo around them, making it hard to tell if anything was following the pair. Every so often, they would stop and listen, but all they could hear was the sound of the cold air and the rushing water they were following meeting their eardrums.

As they walked, the fog grew even denser, until it was almost impossible to see anything at all. Arthur and Caleb slowed their pace, their hearts now pounding in their chests. They had no idea where they were or which way to go.

Suddenly, they heard a low growling sound, and both of them froze. The pack had finally found them. They could hear the animals moving through the fog, their eyes once more glowing in the growing darkness.

Arthur and Caleb drew their weapons, ready to now fight for their lives. They knew that they had to be careful, as the wolves were smart and could easily outmaneuver them in this fog.

As Arthur clocked his rifle, and Caleb Loaded his two hand guns. They looked at each other with readiness.

"Are you ready kid, this is it". Arthur asked as he held his ground.

"Yeah let's take these son's of bitches down". Caleb said before letting out a battle cry out of his lungs that echoed through the Alaskan woods.

Arthur was quick to join his friend, and screamed at the top of his lungs before they both charged to the pack that was already running towards them.

This was it. Their final cry, their final test, their final battle.

Chapter Nine:

The Final Battle

*A*rthur and Caleb charged towards the pack of eye's that were now in the heavy scattered fog, with their weapons in hand. Arthur carried his rifle, while Caleb had his two handguns in each palm. As they continued to run towards the pack, they could start to see an endless sea of wolves stretching out before them as they moved through the heavy mist. The howls of the wolves echoed through the cold Alaskan air, and the smell of fear was as thick as the fur of the hounds that had been tormenting them all this time.

Arthur, and Caleb had encountered the wolves before, but never in such large numbers. Arthur understood that they needed to act quickly and decisively if they were going to survive. Caleb, on the other hand, was still a teen who was accustomed to the many struggles that these woods had thrown his way over the year's. but still he was a young teen who now found himself fed-up with trying to survive, and just wanted to live.

As they got even closer to the pack, Arthur could see the fierce determination in Caleb's eyes. He knew that his friend was ready to give it everything he had, just as he was. The wolves were getting closer now, and Arthur could see the glint of their razor teeth in the upcoming moonlight.

Without hesitation, Arthur and Caleb opened fire. The sound of their gunfire filled the air, and the first row of wolves howled in pain. But there were still too many of them, and they kept on coming. Arthur and Caleb fought with all their might, but they saw they were quickly becoming overwhelmed.

Still Arthur and Caleb stood their ground, but put themselves back to back, their weapons still shooting as they faced the sea of snarling wolves that had now encircled them. The air was combined with the stench of wet fur and drool, and the sound of snapping jaws that now reverberated through the already dimming day that was turning into night.

Arthur gripped his rifle tighter, his heart pounding in his ears as he scanned the pack for any sign of weakness. Caleb, the young and focused teen, stood determined at his back, his two handguns still steady in his palms.

The wolves were closing in even further, their eyes still glowing in the darkness like bright fiery orbs. Arthur took the time to aim and fire, the deafening crack of his rifle splitting the air. The bullet found its mark, striking another wolf in the chest and sending it tumbling to the ground.

Caleb in return fired his handguns in rapid succession, the muzzle flashed lighting up the night as he took down wolf after wolf. But there were still an insurmountable trail of them, and they kept coming, their teeth bared and their eyes fixed on their prey.

Arthur and Caleb fought with everything they had, their weapons blazing as they battled for their lives. They moved with a deadly grace, dodging and weaving through the packs attacks as they fired their weapons with deadly accuracy.

But the wolves were ever so relentless, and their sheer numbers were still overwhelming the pair. Arthur suddenly felt a sharp pain in his bad leg as a wolf sank its teeth into his flesh, and he cried out in agony. Caleb saw his friend go down and realized that they were now in serious trouble.

Caleb shot the beast in the head quickly saving his friend before turning his focus on the others who now saw this opportunity and were now blazing their way towards them with a strict intent to kill.

He fired his remaining ammunition he had on his person, left at the wolves, taking down several more before his guns fell silent. Then he turned to Arthur, who was bleeding heavily from his reopened wounds.

"We need to get out of here!" Caleb shouted, grabbing Arthur's arm and quickly pulling him to his feet. With his free hand he shot his crossbow, but had to drop it as it was too heavy to reload while holding up his friend. So together, they ran away for their lives, the wolves now hot on their heels.

Arthur groaned in pain as Caleb held him up in his arms, his leg bleeding profusely from the bite. They needed to lose these deadly animals. He knew they needed to keep running for their safety, they needed to hold on with every string of their unwavering spirits.

"Kid wait, here take this." Arthur handed the boy a fresh handgun, and held onto the other he had retrieved for himself as well. Together they loaded them with the remaining ammo Arthur had in his pockets.

"Are you ready?" Arthur asked the boy, and the teen nodded in response in the midst of them running for their lives.

"You know I am." Caleb said as his heart raced while he still felt the weight of his injured friend in his arms. He could hear the wolves closing in behind them, their growls and howls echoing through the cold Alaskan trees. He knew they had to stay moving, or they would be surely torn apart by the pack.

With a newfound burst of adrenaline, Caleb kept sprinting forward, his feet pounding against the forest floor. He clutched his fresh handgun tightly, firing it rapidly at the wolves that now lunged towards them. Arthur gritted his teeth, the pain in his leg making it difficult for him to even keep his balance. But he was still focused to keep up with Caleb, to fight for their very own survival.

As they ran, the wolves seemed to multiply even more in numbers, coming at them from every single possible direction. Caleb fired with unerring accuracy, each shot ringing out through the trees. Arthur firing with his own handgun to aid the boy helped where he could.

"Keep firing," he said, his voice hoarse with pain. "We'll make it out of this alive."

Caleb nodded, his eyes fixed on the unknown path ahead. He continued to fire his weapon, gripping it even tighter with his hand like his life depended on it. Each shot kept on hitting its mark. The wolves fell one by one, but there always seemed to be still more coming.

The forest was now a blur of trees and wolves and gunfire, a never-ending nightmare. Caleb could feel sweat pouring down his face, his muscles straining with the effort of holding up Arthur and firing the handgun. But he refused to give up, refused to let the wolves win.

Finally, after what seemed like an eternity, they burst out of the trees and into a clearing. The wolves snarled and snapped at their heels, but Caleb and Arthur kept trying to find a way out of this mess.

Arthur, was still grimacing heavily from the pain. His leg was a mess of blood and torn fabric. He stumbled repeatedly, his grip on Caleb's arm tightening as he kept on forcing himself to keep on moving.

Caleb, with his heart still full of courage, was doing his best to stay persistent and keep Arthur upright. Even though the boy had courage he could feel himself growing more terrified by each dreaded second, but there was still a determined set to his jaw, his breath coming out in steady puffs of white mist. He dared a glance over his shoulder, his heart pounding in his chest as he knew the sea of glowing eyes in the darkness still chased them from behind.

"We're gonna make it," he said, more to himself than to Arthur. His voice trembled with fear, but there was a steel edge to it. "We're gonna make it."

Behind them, the wolves continued their howls, their eerie chorus singing through the frosty air. They were aware that they were getting closer to their targets. Arthur could practically feel their hot breath on his nape, and his heart like his entire experience in these woods pounded in his chest. He tried to ignore the pain in his leg, focusing on the sight of the end of the clearing up ahead.

But suddenly, Arthur stumbled. His leg giving out beneath him, sending both him and Caleb sprawling into the melting snow. Arthur's grunt of pain was drowned out by the snarls of the wolves, now even closer that their salivating jaws were all he could see on the horizon.

"No!" Caleb cried, pulling Arthur up. "Come on, we're almost there!"

He half-dragged, half-carried Arthur, his young muscles straining under the older man's weight. He too could see the end of the clearing now, the moonlight falling on the melting snowy grounds beneath them, promising safety.

As they got back up, and ran their way towards the end of the clearing, hope flickered in Arthur's heart. Maybe they could lose their pursuers here, he thought. The other end of the forest provided a temporary respite from the claustrophobic numbers of the devilish hounds, allowing them to see their surroundings with more focus despite its density. The moonlight bathed the area in an ethereal glow, revealing the twisted shapes of ancient trees that he couldn't help but notice stood like sentinels.

Caleb's grip on Arthur tightened as he scanned their surroundings for any sign of salvation. The adrenaline continuing to course through his veins made his senses acutely aware of every sound, every movement. But the forest remained eerily silent, as if even nature itself held its breath, anticipating the outcome of this desperate chase.

Determined not to succumb to fear, Arthur summoned every ounce of strength he had left within him. He gritted his teeth against the pain and forced his body to move even faster, relying on Caleb's continued unwavering support. They darted in and out of the trees, their footfalls blending with the rustling of melting snowy leaves and the distant howls of the wolves.

But the pair understood that these wolves had always been relentless, gaining ground on them with every passing second. Their hellish snarls grew closer, their desperate hunger driving them to the brink of madness. The scent of fear had always hung heavy in the air, mingling with the musky odor of the unforgiving wilderness that surrounded them. But still they never gave up, and they were solely focused on doing the only thing either of them knew how to do, and that was survive.

Arthur and Caleb ran as if their lives depended on it, because it really did. The forest blurring around them in a mix of fear and determination.

They were now feeling more at ease as they finally gapped a good distance between them and the endless army, but they were aware that they needed to keep on moving. After a while they took notice that the sounds of the wolves cries grew more distant in the darkness of the woods.

Together as they both took note of this newfound realization, they ran with their sheer determination to stay alive, and conqueror this mighty struggle.

As their race against the pack army continued to progress, they were suddenly struck with dread as they hit a dead-end as they felt their bodies collide with the side of a mountain. Their hearts pounding with the horror of trying to figure out what to do next.

Both Arthur and Caleb cursed as they found themselves trapped at the side of this harsh mountain with no visible escape. Arthur's wounds from the wolf bite were still bleeding copiously, and time was running out. With the rest of the wolf pack army only moments away, they were struggling to find a way out of this life-or-death predicament.

"We have to Climb, it's our only way!" Caleb shouted in a last minute attempt. Which Arthur agreed to, and let his friend know that he was ready despite the pain he could still feel in his leg.

"You go first kid I'm right behind you!" Arthur hollered over the sharp wind's.

"No, you go first you can do it!" Caleb said back to his mentor. But Arthur gave him a look of reassurance that signaled to trust him. Which Caleb reluctantly agreed to.

The teen then hurriedly started to climb with urgency trying to get away before the pack caught up to them.

He climbed the tall unforgiving mountain with all his might. His fingers bleeding by the life grip he was using.

Arthur looked up with admiration as the boy was just high enough up that he would be safe.

"Okay Arthur I'm high enough now, let me lower some paracord to you!" Caleb yelled down the mountain side, but he heard no response in return.

As he peaked down he could see Arthur smiling warmly up at him.

"Arthur come on man we need to hurry!" Caleb shouted back for him to start his turn.

Arthur continued smiling as he unzipped his bag, and pulled out his grenade with purpose.

"Arthur what are you doing!?" Caleb questioned with concern.

"It's okay kid!" Arthur called back with warmth in his voice.

"Arthur no! Come on please you can make it!" Caleb pleaded down crying out desperately.

"It's okay son I promise, be safe okay!" Arthur hollered up, before running with everything he had left in his body back into the woods.

"No Arthur, dammit Arthur no!" Caleb screamed at the top of his lungs crying hysterically pounding the side of the mountain.

Arthur sprinted with his bloodied leg, running with his life feeling complete, and his heart finally full.

"Thank you God, thank you Jesus. I know you're with me heavenly father. Forgive me of my sins, I accept your ways lord. Thank you for being my savior." Arthur said in between strained breaths as he ran towards the never-ending sea of wolves that started to come back into his line of sight.

He unlocked the pin to the handheld explosive as he ran faster screaming at his enemy.

Caleb held his breath tight slowly sobbing as he could no longer see his friend as Arthur had now disappeared back into the dense fog, and hadn't come back.

Before the boy could call out, an explosion consumed the Alaskan forest while Caleb stared on in horror.

"Arthur!" Caleb screamed so hard his vocal cords strained to let the noise release from his body.

Arthur had sacrificed himself for not just his friend, but his brother, his only family that he had left.

Several minutes later once the fog had cleared, and the smoke had lightened, the boy climbed down to search for a possible sign of Arthur.

But once he was on the ground he stood frozen by the sight of Arthur's backpack that the man had left behind.

It was with that single glimpse that Caleb dropped to his knees bursting into a fresh flow of tears.

"Dammit Arthur, Dammit." Caleb said sobbing, and hitting the ground.

His only friend was now a pile of ashes that now danced with the winds. They traveled on a journey beyond life now.

They were on a voyage to meet with God, and reunite with the family Arthur had missed so much.

Just as he was gathering himself and getting the strength to stop crying his eyes out, Caleb heard a rustling in the woods in front of him.

The now lone survivor leaned forward looking past his tears trying to see what it was. His eyes soon got overtaken with a look of fear as he saw the same murderous glow of a wolf's eye's.

The teen stood up, quietly drawing his own knife, and stood his ground. He knew he was ready to fight once again.

"Come on you piece of shit! I'm ready. COME AT ME, COME ON!" The boy yelled at the beast as it slowly appeared before him. Snarling with it's infamous drool, and razor-sharp teeth.

But before the 175-pound monster could react, Caleb ran, and lunged forward at him stabbing it right in the chest.

In response the wolf clamped its jaw into the boy's shoulder, sinking its teeth into his bone causing Caleb to cry out in excruciating pain, and twist his blade further into the animal's chest as the pair were now locked together in a standoff. They were both ready to end this war between man and beast once and for all.

"You aren't going to win this time!" Caleb spoke up as he withdrew his blade, and tried stabbing the wolf once more.

With a primal yell that now echoed through the dense forest, Caleb thrust his knife forward, aiming for the wolf's heart once again. The blade sliced through the air; a lethal arc of silver aimed at the creature's chest. The wolf, sensing the imminent danger, twisted its body mid-stance, attempting to evade the lethal strike. Time seemed to slow as Caleb's blade met resistance, scraping against the wolf's fur and scraping past its ribcage.

The wolf's jaws remained locked onto Caleb's shoulder; its grip unyielding despite the pain it had just endured. Blood mingled with the dirt, and melting snow creating a macabre tableau of violence and survival. Caleb's vision blurred, his body trembling with a mix of exhaustion and the primal instinct to survive.

Desperation fueled Caleb's determination. He refused to succumb to the overwhelming amounts of pain that radiated through his body. Summoning every ounce of strength, he wrenched his arm free from the wolf's relentless jaws, leaving behind a shredded mess of torn flesh. The taste of his own blood filled his mouth, his senses heightened by the brutality of the encounter.

Caleb's breath was ragged, his movements sluggish as he struggled to maintain his footing. Blood loss weakened him, threatening to pull him into the abyss of unconsciousness. But he fought against the encroaching darkness, his eyes narrowing in a final act of defiance.

The wolf, sensing the vulnerability of its prey, lunged again, aiming to sink its teeth into Caleb's exposed throat. But Caleb, driven by a primal instinct, and his own unwhielding faith countered with a desperate final strike. With a surge of adrenaline, he redirected his failing strength, driving the blade of his knife deep into the wolf's chest.

A guttural growl escaped the wolf's maw, blending with Caleb's agonized cry. The creature's grip finally loosened, its life force ebbing away.

It was with that final gasp of its last breath that the beast fell in defeat, taking Caleb with it to the ground.

Their blood mixing together into the melting snow was like a blank canvas being painted by a sea of red. It's crimson color creating a memory of horrific proportions that the woods would never forget.

Caleb could feel his body trembling with his exhaustion, while he laid next to the fallen predator. His own blood drenched his torn clothing, the metallic scent of death filling his nostrils. The forest seemed to exhale with the tension dissipating with the life of the last wolf. But Caleb knew the battle was not over. He had to hold onto his life, he had to live.

Just as Caleb could feel the weight of unconsciousness overtake him, he felt his body suddenly being lifted, but didn't have the strength to open his eye's.

If it was death that was greeting him Caleb would not deny it, but accept his fate if it was truly God's will.

"Damn kid I thought you said we can't make dumbass decisions out here." He heard the familiar chuckle.

"Arthur." Caleb whispered softly.

"It's okay kid just rest. We're almost there, you did good." He heard Arthur reassure him.

And it was just like that, Caleb could release his worries, and rested in the arms of his mentor. He only had the energy to listen to the sounds of Arthur's boots trudging through the wood's.

The fight was over, the war was over, and the fear was replaced by a calming sense of peace.

Chapter Ten:

The Will to Survive

As he heard the harmonious beeping of the pulse oximeter fill his ears, Caleb's eyes began to flutter open, the sterile white walls and harsh lighting of the hospital room blinding him momentarily. His throat felt raw, and he struggled to draw a full breath, the oxygen cannula on his nose was cold and uncomfortable. A dull ache radiated from his shoulder, and he winced as he tried to move it. Images of the last wolf lunging toward him filled his mind, and he shuddered by the haunting memory.

As he lay there on the cold thin white sheets, he tried to piece together the events of the past few years he had gone through, but as he was doing so, a nurse entered the room. Where she checked his vitals and adjusted his oxygen.

"How are you feeling today, Caleb?" she asked, her voice gentle and soothing.

Caleb blinked, trying to focus on her words. "I don't know," he mumbled. "My shoulder still hurts, and I can't really remember everything. How do you know my name?" Caleb questioned with his nerves still on high alert for the moment.

The nurse nodded sympathetically in understanding the teens current state of confusion. "It's normal to feel confused after a traumatic event. But don't worry, your memory will come back in time. We know you from the local authorities board we have here. Your name is Caleb Cane. You were presumed dead about six year's ago. Everyone searched around the area where you and your father were last seen. After 90 day's local law enforcement called the search off. When you were brought in here, we had to run a DNA test to confirm your identity as it's now necessary within our state requirements."

Once the nurse was done explaining the situation, she left Caleb to adjust to her words.

While he sat there in his hospital bed, Caleb was left to adjust to the information he had just been told about himself.

Everyone had been looking for him, but had suddenly just given up. It was the final nail that Caleb had been set in place for what would lead this teen on the next events of his already harsh life.

As a few hours had now passed, Caleb sat there lost deep in thought, when the same nurse walked into his room. "Caleb, there's someone here to see you," she said with another warm smile.

Caleb looked up and saw a mysterious man in a firefighter's uniform standing in the doorway. "Hi Sir, it's good to see you're awake," the man said, while walking over to the bed.

Caleb was confused as he didn't recognize this person. "I'm sorry, who are you?"

The man smiled. "My name is Mike Lee. I'm the paramedic who found you in the woods. My unit saw the smoke and got orders to respond. When we arrived we found you. You were in really bad shape."

Caleb's eyes widened in surprise as a memory had hit him. "But I thought it was my mentor Arthur who saved me."

Mike shook his head. "I'm sorry, but you were the only one we found out there. We didn't see no signs of anyone else." Mike said looking on at the teen as he struggled to come to terms with the man's words.

"Thank you, Mike," Caleb said, his voice filled with a new wave of grief hitting him.

Mike smiled with a sympathetic look. "You're welcome, Caleb. Just doing my job." He paused for a moment before adding, "I'm sorry we couldn't find your friend."

Caleb nodded, feeling too overwhelmed with emotion to even give a reply.

As his vision cleared and his memories slowly returned, Caleb finally remembered Arthur, his word's in the woods. But had it really been Arthur? The firefighter who had found him after the explosion – he was the one who must-have carried him to safety, not Arthur. The realization kept hitting Caleb like a tidal wave, and he couldn't hold back the sobs that wracked his already frail body.

Arthur was really gone. Dead. And Caleb was still alone.

After a short time Police officers entered the room, their faces etched with concern and curiosity. They questioned him about the events in the woods, trying to piece together what had happened. Caleb did his best to recount the story, but his voice was weak, and his thoughts were consumed by the loss of his mentor.

Social services arrived as well, explaining that they would be taking Caleb into protective care once he was well enough.

The teen listened numbly as they detailed their plans, his heart heavy with grief. But as they prepared to leave, he noticed a small, crumpled piece of paper on the bedside table by his bag. The handwriting was unmistakably Arthur's, and it bore a single word: Survive.

Caleb clutched the paper tightly in his hand, his resolve igniting like a spark in the darkness. With a sudden burst of energy, he tore the oxygen cannula from his face and swung his legs over the side of the bed. Ignoring the pain in his shoulder, he slipped past the startled social workers and made a break for the door.

As Caleb sprinted down the hospital corridors, his heart pounded in his chest, both from exertion and the determination that coursed through his veins. Arthur may have been gone, but his memory lived on in Caleb, and he would honor his mentor by surviving, no matter what challenges lay ahead.

Outside the hospital, the crisp Alaskan air stung Caleb's lungs, but he didn't slow down. He was free, and he knew he had to keep moving. Though grief weighed heavily on his heart, he was ready to fight for his survival once more. For Arthur, for him, And for life.

Caleb vanished into the shadows of the day, a young teen on a journey to honor his mentor and find his own strength in a world that had taken so much from him. The road ahead would be long and arduous, but Caleb was ready to face it, armed with the will to survive and the memory of Arthur guiding him every step of the way.

A few day's earlier…

Arthur was running with the grenade in hand pulling off the pin with an expression of determination, and content.

Just as he was about to throw it he saw a small trench a few feet away in the ground, and without a second to spare he threw himself into it as he flung the explosive at the army of wolves headed his direction.

Before the man could cover his ears, an explosion consumed the air above him as he screamed his lungs out.

After the explosion was over Arthur peaked his way out of the trench to see if the coast was clear.

As he stood up, he could see all the wolves were burnt to a crisp into the melted snow.

Arthur limped his way to one of them as he towered over it in victory. "Fuck you." Arthur mumbled spitting on it's lifeless body.

He then ripped off his sleeve to his winter jacket, and used it as a tourniquet to finally stop his bleeding on his injured leg.

As he turned to make his way back to Caleb he Could hear the sound of a fight ensuing.

He sprinted as best as he could, back to Caleb, but as he approached the scene, he could see the fight was already over.

Arthur rushed over to his friend where he checked for a pulse. He sighed with relief when he saw the boy was indeed alive.

Gingerly Arthur lifted the boy into his arms, and proceeded to carry him through the woods.

He smiled to himself as he remembered the joke Caleb would tell him. "Damn kid I thought we weren't supposed to make dumbass decisions out here." Arthur said aloud laughing.

"Arthur." He heard the boy whisper.

"It's okay kid just rest. We're almost there, you did good." Arthur said reassuring him to relax as he limped carrying the boy to safety.

While he struggled with the weight of carrying Caleb with a bad leg, Arthur started to hear something on the vast horizon.

He stopped momentarily to listen closely, and as he focused he could hear the sound of the familiar blades of a helicopter.

Arthur sprinted forward with the boy in his arms as he could hear it getting closer. Once he found himself in a clearing, Arthur could see the helicopter attempting to land.

He looked down at the boy and set him down where the paramedics could find him. Arthur then took out a pencil he had in his pocket with a piece of paper, and quickly wrote survive on it.

Once the note was tucked into Caleb's pocket, Arthur walked away into the darkness of the forest.

He didn't want to leave the boy, but he knew it was the best for him. Caleb was a strong young man that would turn out well one day.

However, Arthur understood that it was best if he only looked out for Caleb from a distance rather than up close.

As Arthur approached his own bag, and was about to swing it over his shoulder he noticed a piece of paper sticking out of the back pocket.

He opened it as he saw the chopper back in the air flying off into the good night sky.

Dear Arthur,

I hope this letter finds you well. I wanted to take a moment to express my deepest gratitude for all that you have done for me over the past few months. Your bravery and presence saved my life when I was in a dire situation just like I did with you, and for that, I will be forever grateful.

But beyond that, I want you to know how much your friendship means to me. You have been more than just a friend to me, you have been my family. Your unwavering support and guidance have helped me through some of the toughest moments of my life. I cannot imagine where I would be without you.

As we move forward, I am uncertain about what the future holds as we go onto this journey, and how we might encounter the wolves. But what I do know is that you will always be my best friend. Your kindness, loyalty, and love have made an indelible mark on my heart, and I will carry it with me always.

Thank you for being you, Arthur. I am blessed to call you my friend, but even more my brother.

Sincerely,

Caleb.

As Arthur refolded the note and placed it in his pocket, he smiled looking off into the distance.

"See you around kid." Arthur said before putting his backpack on, and walking off again into the woods where he was setting out onto his next journey.

This wasn't the end by any means, but it was just the beginning. The beginning of an even greater story to be told.

Postface

While I sit here reflecting on the journey that was Surviving The Pack, I am reminded of the emotional weight that came with telling the story of Arthur and Caleb. It was not an easy task, as I found myself grappling with the pain and suffering that these two survivors had experienced. Their struggles were all too familiar to me, as I too face emotional and spiritual challenges on a daily basis.

Yet, even in the face of such hardships, Arthur and Caleb never gave up. They persevered, fought through their pain, and emerged on the other side stronger and more resilient than ever before. It was a truly poetic journey, one that reminded me of the importance of never losing sight of the light, even in our darkest moments.

As I wrote about Arthur and Caleb's experiences, I couldn't help but draw a few parallels to my own life. Their struggles were a reflection of my own, and their triumphs were a source of hope and inspiration.

I am grateful for the opportunity to have told their story, and I hope that it serves as a reminder to all who read it that no matter how difficult life may seem, there is always hope. We must never give up, even when the odds seem stacked against us. For it is in these moments of darkness that we must focus on the light, and emerge stronger and more resilient than ever before.

Character bio's

ARTHUR PETERS

Arthur Peters is a man who has faced more than his fair share of challenges in life. A
widower who lost his wife in a car accident as well as their son in the same tragedy found Arthur with nothing but his grief and pain.

As a result of these losses, Arthur withdrew from society and turned towards survivalism as a way of coping with his pain. He spends most of his time in the wilderness, honing his skills and preparing for any eventuality. His face bears the scars of a life lived hard, weathered by the elements and marked by sorrow.

Despite his isolation, Arthur has a deep and abiding connection to his faith. He finds solace in prayer and meditation, and believes that his survivalist lifestyle is a way of living in harmony with God's creation. He is always ready for whatever challenges life may throw his way, and he faces them with a quiet determination that speaks to his strength of character.

However, Arthur's struggles with suicidal thoughts are a constant battle. He has moments of despair when he wonders whether life is worth living, whether the pain of his losses will ever ease. But he clings to his faith and his survivalist training as a lifeline, and somehow manages to find the strength to keep going.

In his early 40s, Arthur Peters is a man who has been through more than most people could imagine. But his resilience and determination in the face of adversity are a testament to the human spirit, and a reminder that even in the darkest of times, there is always hope.

CALEB
CANE

Caleb Cane is a teenage survivalist who has been living in the wilderness for six years. He was thrust into this lifestyle when a trip with his dad went horribly wrong, resulting in a tragic car accident that left his dad dead. Caleb was left alone in the wilderness, constantly on the run from a persistent pack of wolves and other predators in the Alaskan wilderness.

Despite the harsh reality of his situation, Caleb has managed to survive through sheer determination and resourcefulness. He has become an expert at building shelters, finding food and water, and evading danger. His gray eyes betray the pain and trauma he has endured, but his quick wit and sarcastic sense of humor serve as a tool to mask his pain.

Living in the wilderness has forced Caleb to grow up quickly and he has adapted to the harsh realities of his surroundings. He is a skilled hunter and gatherer, and has become adept at reading the signs of the wilderness. Despite his rugged exterior, Caleb has a soft spot for nature, and has even formed a bond with the land of the Alaskan woods.

Caleb's experiences have left him with a deep sense of self-reliance and a fierce independence. He is a survivor in every sense of the word, and his experiences have shaped him into a formidable force to be reckoned with

To my readers,

I would like to take a moment to express my heartfelt gratitude for taking the time to read "Surviving The Pack". It has been an incredible experience, and I feel truly blessed to have had the opportunity to share this story with you.

Writing this book has been a passion project of mine, and I am so grateful that you have trusted me to provide you with a story that I hope you enjoyed as much as I did. Your feedback and support have been invaluable, and it is because of you that I have been able to continue writing and am able to share this with the world.

I want to thank you from the bottom of my heart for being a part of this journey. Your support means everything to me, and I will forever be grateful for you the readers who have come along for the ride.

Thank you again for your trust in me and for reading "Surviving The Pack". I hope that it has brought you as much joy and entertainment as it has brought me in writing it.

With gratitude,

Rafael Garcia.

In Memory Of Carlos Garcia

January 1st 1942 – August 2nd 2000

Acknowledgments

For this being my first book, I'd like to take a moment, and acknowledge the following people who have supported and inspired my journey. If it weren't for these outstanding individuals this book would not have been possible to have the strength to write.

- Yvonne M Garcia.
- Rosalinda Garcia.
- Arlene Womble.
- Steven Womble.
- Mykel Womble.
- Makayla Womble.
- Ricardo Garcia.
- Christin Garcia.
- Richard Garcia.
- Amelia Garcia
- Alvaro Ramirez.
- Natasha Ramirez.
- Peyton Ramirez.
- Jet Ramirez.
- Sara-Lee Hutto.
- Michael Boyer.
- Michael Womble.
- Cheryl Womble.
- Alicia Muraida.
- Edward Muraida.

- Rosemary Tavitas.
- Michael Tavitas.

- Larry Resendez.
- Idalia Resendez.

- Linda Bequette.
- Bobby Hutto.

- Mark Tovar.
- Kat Tovar.

- Heather Malcolm.
- Melanie Petrash.

- Greg Harmon.
- Stephanie Duke.

- Yolanda Sims.
- Angela Moss

- Angie Billingsley.
- Julie Clark.

- Katie Graham Stone.
- George Dewberry.

- George Carey.
- Jenna Medlock.

- Kenneth Johnson.
- Alex Gutierrez.

- Casey Divin.
- Randall Bell.

- Hector Suarez.
- Mary L Suarez.

- Carlos Garcia Jr.
- Cindy M Garcia.
- Sylvia G Teniente.
- Manuel Teniente.
- Cynthia Garcia.
- Lucia Morales.
- Roberto Garcia.
- Sandra Garcia.
- Gloria Suarez.
- Janel Hernandez.
- Steven Kalter.
- Melvin Smith.
- Earl Stanley.
- Robert Zajac.
- Terry Pick.
- Daniel Garcia
- Richard Hernandez.
- Roman Hernandez
- Aldo Parodi.
- James Andry.
- Elizabeth Gonzalez.
- Jacob Gonzalez.
- Tobi Brown.
- Bennie Jones.
- Patrick Stewart.
- Alejandra Stewart.

- David Hinojosa.
- Ricardo Scott.

- Shasta Stiles.
- Margaret Adams.

- Jacob Ortiz.
- Apolonia Elizondo.

- Judy Cho.
- Bryan J Kelly.

- Tony Schiavone.
- Shaun O'Neal.

- Ralph Xavier.
- Noah Sims.

- Chelsea Lira.
- Stewart Lira.

- Luca Manfè.
- Austin Gunn.

- Justin Robert's.
- Rey Paez.

- Cesar Cano.
- Chandra Smith.

- Jennifer Lindsay.
- Billy Gunn.

- Alex Garcia.
- Corey D Samuel's.

- Krystle Starr.
- Hetal Vasavada.

- Anthony Ogogo.   • Blake Chadwick.

- Kyle Herbert.   • Brian King Joseph.

- Manny Garcia.   • Brielle Baker.

- Boone Langston. • Dino Luciano.

- Yachecia Jarmon. • Francis Legge.

- Aaron Newman.   • Derrick Fox.

- Monti Carlo.   • Brandi Alexander.

Katnia DeJarnett.   • Randy Santel.

- Bobby Cruise.   • Ernie Zuniga.

- Adam Caskey.   • Isiah Kassidy.

- Chuck Miketinac. • Edgar Delgado.

- Gerron Hurt.   • Carol Del Los Santos.

- Jeannine Camacho.

Coming Soon

The dimly lit room of the Cabin's basement was filled with an eerie silence, punctuated by the thug's labored breaths. Bounded to a wooden chair, his wrists tightly secured behind his back, he squirmed in desperation, his eyes darting around the room for a glimmer of hope. Beads of sweat and blood trickled down his forehead, his unkempt hair clinging to his face. Fear and uncertainty etched deep lines across his features.

"P-please," he stammered, his voice trembling with a mixture of fear and desperation. "I don't know anything. You've got the wrong guy I swear!"

But his pleas fell on deaf ears. The footsteps only grew louder, resonating with a sense of purpose. The thug's heart pounded in his chest, a cacophony of dread. He strained against his restraints more, the ropes biting into his skin deeper, as the room's heavy stairs creaked with each heavy step.

A tall, shadowy figure stepping into the room, his presence radiating an aura of authority. His face obscured by the darkness of the shadows, only the glint of cold, calculating eyes was visible. The thug's breath hitched in his throat as he recognized the voice of his attacker that followed.

"I'm going to ask you one more time," the man's voice was low, resonant, each word dripping with a chilling determination. "Where is Caleb?"

The thug's mind raced, trying to make sense of the name. Caleb? Who was Caleb? He had no knowledge of any Caleb, and yet his life depended on providing an answer.

"I swear, I don't know any Caleb!" he cried out, his voice laced with desperation. "I'm just a hired hand. They didn't tell me anything!"

The man's eyes narrowed, his gaze piercing through the darkness. He took a deliberate step closer, his footsteps echoing off the cold, wooden floor. The thug's heart skipped a beat. He had no choice but to reveal the truth, even if it meant putting himself at risk.

"Wait!" he exclaimed, a glimmer of realization dawning on him. "I'll…… I'll tell you, I'll tell you everything you need to know."

"Oh I know you are, because we're about to go on one hell of a ride." Arthur said pointing his handgun at the thug's face before clicking back the hammer of his weapon ready to fire.

Arthur and Caleb

Will Return in Critical Point.